Second Chance Dance

AN ENEMIES TO LOVERS HISTORICAL ROMANCE

BARTHOLOMEW SERIES
BOOK TWO

LANEY HATCHER

Copyright

This book is a work of fiction. Any resemblance to actual persons, living or dead or undead, events, locales is entirely coincidental.

Copyright © 2022 by Laney Hatcher; All rights reserved.

No part of this book may be reproduced, scanned, photographed, or distributed in any printed or electronic form without explicit written permission from the author.

Made in the United States of America

Developmental Edits: Nicole McCurdy, Emerald Edits
Editing: Julia Ganis, JuliaEdits.com
Cover Illustration: Blythe Russo
Proofreading: Judy's Proofreading

One

MILES

London, 1856

Some things never changed.

Taking in the grandeur and general splendor of Lady Hawkesberry's ballroom, I realized how stagnant and unchanging society truly was.

I'd been away for six years, and yet it was as if I'd never left.

Though their faces and names had changed, wallflowers still gathered along the edge of the ballroom in their pastel dresses. Elegant matrons still congregated in packs, waving their fans and spreading the latest gossip. Marriage-mad mamas still dragged their offspring from introduction to introduction in an effort to produce a sound match.

And the season was just beginning.

I absentmindedly tugged at the shirt cuffs beneath my black jacket, searching the crowd for a friendly face. Those, too, had hardly changed. Perhaps a bit more mature, with lined creases near their eyes, but familiar nonetheless. After a moment I spotted a group of young bucks—or they had been years ago—conversing near the open balcony doors, drinks in hand.

Thomas Faulk, the Viscount Finnigan, caught my approach and, eyes widening comically, called out, "Basilton! You're alive!"

I offered a laughing smile as the gathered gentlemen turned. Their surprised shouts and greetings were drawing attention. Yet I couldn't claim shock. I'd been gone a long time. After a rather scandalous forced departure from England, I'd had little to no contact with these men—ones I'd long known from shared circumstances and the ever-present consistency in ballrooms.

Thomas shook my hand and provided a jovial clap on the shoulder. "What the devil happened to you, Basil?"

I returned the shake but ignored the question. "Finnigan, good to see you."

We'd been friendly at Eton and ran in the same circles at university as well. Thomas's question was derailed and overlooked as gentlemen from the past made themselves reacquainted with me in the present. Hearty back slaps and well-wishes all around.

Ebenezer Petty, the Marquess of Caldwell, gave my hand a firm squeeze. "Welcome back, Basilton. Are you in London for the whole season, then?"

My smile was genuine. I'd always gotten on well with Caldwell. "Indeed I am."

"Time to settle down and assume the role of heir. Is that what's brought you back to England?"

Eb's words were innocent and curious, but they caused something to twist bitterly behind my ribs. And following my warm welcome, those assembled—and even more within earshot—were eager for my response. They didn't know the complexity of what I'd been asked. They couldn't realize the mixed feelings I had regarding my return.

Before I could be assaulted by complicated memories and ultimatums, I turned back to my former friends and addressed the unavoidable. "You are correct, Caldwell. Seems I'm getting a little long in the tooth." They laughed, as I intended. For thirty years an earl did not a spinster make. I was merely a bachelor—accepted in status, even for an heir responsible for continuing the line. "Time for me to take my place in polite society," I confirmed.

They didn't need to know the extent of my intentions—or lack thereof. I'd participate in this season. I'd dance in ballrooms. I'd paint the picture of a dashing gentleman. I'd do just enough to get by and not draw attention to myself. All so I could come home.

"That's the spirit," said Lord Pritchard, a gentleman around my age who'd been circulating these same ballrooms for a decade.

"There comes a time for us all," agreed Ebenezer.

"Is that so?" I asked in good humor. "I don't see a pretty wife on your arm, Caldwell."

He laughed at my teasing. "Ah, yes. Well, perhaps this season will be promising for us all." With a pointed look behind me, the gentlemen in our loose circle cast sly, knowing glances and huffed amused chuckles under their breath.

My eyes narrowed. "What am I missing?"

Another voice from my past took the opportunity to speak up and explain. "That's right, Basilton. You've been away too long," Simon Edgemoore said, tone laced with amusement. "The catch of this season and the last is just behind you. She's a rather un-merry widow but her fortune is legendary. And she threw down an exceedingly tempting gauntlet last year at a crowded event when she declared haughtily that she'd never marry again." Several men laughed. "The lady didn't anticipate what a challenge she has presented, and there is a bit of a gentleman's wager on who will be the one to land her."

That sounded like more trouble than it was worth.

The six acquaintances surrounding me looked on expectantly. "I see," was the only reply I could think to make. Honestly, I was having an exceedingly difficult time mustering any enthusiasm for this conversation and those speaking. I felt more removed from these men—my former friends—than ever.

If I'd thought my return to society would be like sliding on a familiar glove, well, apparently I'd been mistaken. The fit wasn't quite right, after all.

"Well, what do you say?" asked Thomas Faulk. "Care to throw in your lot? Join the wager and bag your future wife. It is why you're back in London, is it not?"

These men didn't know why I was back in London, but they could continue thinking it was for all the respectable reasons an heir resumes his place in society. The twisting frustration threatened once more as thoughts of my father rose on the horizon.

Attempting levity and pushing my mounting anger away, I glanced around me and smiled. "Right you are, Finnigan. I'll join your wager and apply myself to wooing this unhappy widow with gusto."

In truth I'd already put the idea out of my head. I definitely didn't care enough to inquire after the woman's identity. And when the Marquess Daly—someone whose company I'd always enjoyed—broke ranks and interrupted our discussion, I hardly noticed at all. I bid the intrepid gamblers a good evening and joined Daly on the balcony for a brandy and that was that.

∼

"So Kendrick died in a brawl?"

Daly winced. "Yes, last year. Bad business at a card table. His brother—Augustus, you remember him—inherited and married shortly after."

I took a sip of amber liquid and racked my brain trying to remember the Ward family lineage and the current Duke of Kendrick.

"He's younger than you. Augie was at Cambridge with me. He's a good sort. You'd like him, and his duchess is a good match. She gives him a harder time than I do." Daly smiled, his green eyes crinkling genuinely.

I nodded. "I think Augustus and I were introduced before—well, years ago." I would forever be stumbling over the last six years of my life.

The evening was mild. With the torches on the balcony and stairs leading to the gardens, the setting was fairly idyllic. And with Daly's company, I could have some measure of peace. While the circle of gentlemen within had greeted me wholeheartedly, most society members in attendance hadn't yet placed me. In the years I'd been in France—in my exile—I'd grown and matured. The journey to manhood had given me a different outlook and a new outward appearance. My perpetual baby face had lost the softness of youth, and my lean stature had taken to regular exercise in the boxing ring as well as an interest in equestrian pursuits.

It was strange to be back with this indistinguishable yet altered appearance. Those previous acquaintances had recognized me easily enough. Perhaps I was the only one who felt so transformed. And admittedly, I hadn't been in the ballroom very long before being drawn into conversation with Caldwell and Finnigan and the others. I felt confident that chins would be wagging upon my return from the balcony. But surely my scandalous past behavior had been long forgotten. Undoubtedly more gossip-worthy deeds had overshadowed my uneasy exit from polite society all those years ago.

"Well, I'm off for another drink," Daly said, pushing away from the terrace's stone railing. "And I should probably take a few turns about the dance floor."

I nodded. "Good to see you, Daly."

"Welcome home, Basil."

I stared out over the gardens as his retreating footsteps carried him back to the ballroom. I should return as well. My mother was here somewhere. I was sure there were introductions and re-introductions to be made.

Six years was a long time. But in some ways, not long enough.

Moving farther down the balcony, toward the encroaching darkness, I found a table to place my empty glass on and resolved myself to reentering the merriment. But before I could take a step toward the open doorway, a woman burst out onto the terrace. I froze from my place some yards away and remained quiet. Shrouded in darkness as I was, I didn't mean to frighten her. Perhaps she'd move toward the stairs and be on her way, and I could be on mine.

But she didn't. She took a deep breath and moved closer, farther along the railing before approaching the stone barrier and bracing her hands. I took in her stooped posture. Her form was hunched in defeat or frustration—it was hard to know. She didn't appear to be crying, thank God for that. That was all I needed—a hysterical woman trapping me outside for who knew how long.

I observed her a moment longer, hoping she'd find her composure and return inside. But she remained, arms braced, gazing on the stone pavers beneath her elegant slippers. Even in the darkness and waning warm torchlight, I could see her hair was pale blond and elaborate in its adornment. An elegant tiara shone from her crown. The exact shade of her dress eluded me but it was patterned and jeweled and every other thing a fashionable young lady might wear. But this woman before me was no newly out society miss. As I took in her gloved hands still pressing into the stone and the tense expression pinching her features, it was clear she was just a few years my junior.

She was rather lovely. Objectively. Had I been *actually* in the market for a countess, I might have politely cleared my throat and introduced myself. Or comforted her and asked after the circumstances that forced her from the ballroom.

But I wasn't. And my charms were not required. I simply needed to leave.

I'd remained too long without announcing my presence, but there was nothing for it. I would make this awkward and then be on my way.

However, before I could manage a cough, the delicate creature before me clenched her jaw and gritted out a "Fucking arsehole" beneath her breath and a laugh escaped me instead.

Her head whipped in my direction. She was the furthest thing from startled or alarmed by my presence. This lady's expression could have scorched the face of the earth with its fire. It certainly melted the unexpected amusement from mine.

"Apologies," I offered. "I was in the corner"—I pointed to the table and low chair behind me—"when you arrived."

She said nothing, but by some unholy force of nature, her glare managed to intensify. So I kept talking lest flames erupt from her mouth.

"And then I waited to see if you'd proceed to the gardens." My clarification elicited no response. And my mouth apparently could not afford me the same favor. "But then you remained and I didn't know how to announce my presence without frightening you."

That finally did it because one elegant brow rose. "Do I appear frightened?"

"Not in the least," I said with a grin.

Her gaze narrowed and did a quick sweep of my form. There was no recognition to be found on either side. For if I had met this woman during my years in London, I would have remembered it. A woman who cursed with a mouth like that. Nothing if not memorable.

Amusement threatened again as I recalled the unexpected profanity she'd uttered. She was wild, this one. And fearless. Most women would be startled by an unexpected man invading a private moment. Even at a ball in Mayfair, an unknown gentleman could still very well be a threat. But this lady seemed merely annoyed.

"Do you mind me asking," I continued despite her answering glare, "to which fucking arsehole were you referring? You see, I'm newly to town, so I'd like to avoid any unpleasant encounters."

Her countenance hardly changed but I detected something alter in her posture. "You're new to town?"

The voice was still steely and offered nothing on her thoughts beyond her question.

"I am indeed. I've spent my time in France for the most part, but have returned to London for the season." When she made no move to respond, I decided to engage further. This was getting fun. And Miles Griffin, the Earl of Basilton, was never one to turn down a little of that. "So. Was it a man? I'm sure it was. No one ever calls a lady a 'fucking arsehole.' And honestly, if someone deserved that particular nomenclature, it would be a male, I'm sure."

"Is that so?" she inquired, gaze still penetrating. And if she was free to stare so openly, I wouldn't be passing up the opportunity either.

She was backlit by the torches and her features weren't entirely clear but she was gorgeous, to be sure. When she'd first arrived on the balcony, her profile had been twisted in anger. The beauty had been secondary to her expression. But now that I could see more than just frustration, her face and figure were a sight to behold. There was something a little familiar about her as well, but I'd been feeling that way about nearly everyone I'd come in contact with since my return.

"It is so," I finally answered. "I'm fairly confident you're maligning a scoundrel —perhaps a rake who deserved it. With utmost assurance, you called a man— likely in that ballroom—a fucking arsehole."

"Stop saying 'fucking arsehole,'" she snapped.

"Why? Are you the only one allowed to say it?" I retorted with a beaming smile.

Unmoved by the charm I'd wielded so easily, she asked abruptly, "Who are you?"

I glanced beyond the mystery woman toward the light spilling from the ballroom and the strains of music providing the background sounds to this unexpected encounter. She didn't seem at all worried about being discovered unchaperoned with me out here. "Who are *you*?" I countered.

Her lip twitched, and I felt confident enough to exaggerate that expression and call it a smile. "How long have you been in France?"

"Six years," I answered quickly. It was fairly common knowledge. She could find out easily enough. And for some reason I didn't feel the resentful pinch that typically accompanied talk of my time abroad. I found our banter too diverting… and enjoyable. If my quick responses kept up our game, then I would play along.

Upon my admission, the lady's eyes lost focus and she seemed to consider something before finally replying. "I'm Patricia Henney, the Duchess of Cawthorn."

"A pleasure to make your acquaintance, Your Grace. I am Miles Griffin, the Earl of Basilton." I winked and executed a tidy bow.

I didn't recall her situation, nor her duke. The peerage had hardly held my interest across the Channel during my time away. My bitterness and anger hadn't afforded me the patience nor the interest in those I'd left behind.

Masculine laughter erupted from the doorway beyond, drifting on the night air. The duchess stiffened, but after forcing her shoulders back and meeting my gaze, she said, "A pleasure to meet you as well. Would you care to dance?"

Surprise had my eyebrows jumping. She'd been quite frosty in her countenance this evening despite the fire in her gaze. An invitation to dance had been entirely unexpected and was completely unorthodox. I rather thought she'd be more likely to fling me over the railing for witnessing her moment of vulnerability earlier.

"You want to dance with me?" I pointed to my chest, as if there was some other gentleman out here to be mistaken for.

"I suppose," came her maddening answer.

Her nonchalance made me replay her invitation just a moment prior. She made it sound now as if it hadn't been her idea at all. I frowned. "Why did you say it that way?"

Now she frowned. "What way?"

"I suppose," I mimicked in a high-pitched register. "As if you'd do me this favor of dancing with me."

The duchess's glare was baleful. "I did not say it that way."

"I think you did," I argued for no other reason than to see if she'd break decorum and roll her eyes at my insistence. I bit back a smile as she proved me right. "And furthermore, I am an accomplished dancer. If anyone was bestowing the literal favor of a dance, it would be me."

She sighed as if greatly put-upon and my desire to further irritate her increased tenfold. "I want to dance with someone I do not know. And more importantly… someone who does not know me."

Interesting.

I wasn't sure how to interpret her admission but I figured it had something to do with the fucking arsehole. I considered being used for nothing beyond my recent arrival to town, and then decided I didn't care. I would take this dance and this odd desire to push all of her elegant and fashionable buttons. Perhaps the next time we danced she'd desire it for a different reason.

"Very well, then." Smiling, I approached and offered my arm, coming close enough to see her very perceptive gaze follow my movements. She wasn't intimidated. And she very clearly did not trust me, but whatever the duchess's purpose might be, trust was not something she required.

I let the charming smile I'd attempted fall away as she wrapped her small hand around my arm. My easy manner and friendliness were equally unnecessary for this woman. If her trust and attention were something to be won…well, they wouldn't be achieved with a winning smile. I had a feeling her approval was rarely given and something only ever earned.

Our reentry into the ballroom was well timed. The musicians were just preparing for the waltz as dancers took their positions in the crowded space.

If my companion was concerned with the attention we'd garnered upon our arrival or the whispers that could hardly be contained, she didn't show it. This woman was cool and confident, and seeing her in the bright light of an infinite number of candles was doing something odd to my heartbeat. She'd been objectively beautiful on the darkened terrace. But here, with her cornflower-blue eyes regarding me and her body warm and waiting in my arms, she was otherworldly.

I'd seen and bedded gorgeous women before. This mysterious young duchess should not be causing me anything beyond simple attraction. But my chest was thrumming an inordinate beat.

We danced together as the instruments played. I guided our movements, and still my heart beat with urgency, with knowing. I ignored everyone around us, and despite my tendency to be a quick conversationalist, could no longer utter a single word in her presence.

Her poise and elegance now made the scene I'd witnessed on the balcony feel intrusive. Was that woman outside the true Duchess of Cawthorn or was it the enigma in my arms? For now, she was completely in control and had little notice for anyone else. The fact that I'd seen her outside in such an ungoverned and vulnerable moment made all the amusement I'd felt leach away. I could sense the shift. Her outburst had been personal and private. And I'd been an unwelcome observer. No wonder she'd looked ready to breathe fire.

Something was happening between us now. This dance—this moment—felt heavy with intent. More than the quick quips and banter from the balcony. This was something else entirely.

Finally the music ended, but the spell was far from broken. I offered a polite bow in response to her graceful curtsy.

Swallowing convulsively, I realized I needed to say something. Yet my charms and charisma had abandoned me in the face of this growing awareness.

After a quick glance behind me, the duchess said, "Good evening to you, Basilton."

I finally managed to formulate words. "Yes, to you as well, Your Grace." She started to turn, but urgency propelled me. "Wait." When she paused in her retreat, I realized I hadn't planned how to conclude my thought.

For the first time all night, she looked nearly amused. "Yes, my lord?"

"We should dance again," I blurted as her blond brows rose. "Not tonight, I know that. But another evening. Another event. I should like to dance with you again." This was not appropriate. She was a duchess and potentially married. I didn't know what I was saying, but I knew this couldn't be the last time we spoke.

With a glint in those remarkable blue eyes, Patricia, the Duchess of Cawthorn, replied, "Perhaps that can be arranged." And with that, she removed herself easily from the dance floor while I retreated dazedly and bumped into several faceless individuals.

Aimless and unsettled, I was startled when Thomas Faulk pulled me by the arm back to the circle of gentlemen I'd spoken to earlier. Caldwell was still there, as well as all the others.

"Basil, you sneaky bugger," Thomas accused. "How did you wrangle a dance with the duchess already?"

I was slightly taken aback by their attention, but the men continued on undeterred.

"Basilton is clearly up to snuff, gentlemen. He's out for blood."

"You should definitely be gloating, Basil," Caldwell said. "The duchess hardly ever agrees to a dance with anyone of marriageable age and intent."

I frowned in confusion, but before I could attempt to figure out this asinine conversation, I glanced back to where the Duchess of Cawthorn had retreated near the refreshment table. She was conversing with a tall, red-haired woman I did not recognize but both women were glaring daggers in my direction.

"Well, men, we shall have to up our game. The Earl of Basilton has taken a clear and decisive lead."

I turned away from the duchess's angry stare and snapped, "The lead in what?"

Caldwell's incredulous expression was all I could focus on as he clarified, "In the bet to land the most reluctant lady in London. Patricia Henney, the Duchess of Cawthorn."

The gentlemen let out several cheers as if Caldwell's statement were a call to arms. My mouth dropped open in understanding as the six men enveloped me in congratulatory back slaps. In sudden understanding and frustrated panic, I whipped around in time to see the lady in question storm away from the refreshment table and through a doorway, leaving the red-haired woman to regard me coolly before she followed in her lady's wake.

I couldn't help but think I wouldn't be getting that second dance anytime soon.

A fucking arsehole, indeed.

The gentleman's eyes focused in on me and I straightened. "What a glorious event, is it not?"

"Quite," I agreed, making sure to keep my tone impervious and my demeanor cool. You couldn't give an inch to these lordlings. They'd take a mile. Or attempt to take a fortune.

Unbothered by my unaffected air, Lord Finnigan smiled brightly. "Your Grace, I was hoping to secure your hand…"

My eyes widened. That was a first. None of The Gaggle had come right out and proposed before.

"For a dance," he finished with a wink. As if his efforts and humor would set him apart from the others.

"Apologies, my lord. These slippers are new and my feet are not up to dancing this evening. Perhaps you can attain my wealth…" His jaw dropped. "…of dancing expertise at the next ball," I concluded my statement, sans wink.

After Lord Finnigan coughed awkwardly, he bid us all good night.

"That was cold, Patricia," Mary said. "I loved it."

I allowed a tiny smile to tug the corners of my lips and glanced to Mary and Emery, who gave me sly, wicked grins of their own. As I returned my gaze to the room at large, I caught Miles Griffin looking on in amusement. Our eyes locked and his smile dropped like a swooning miss. I blinked and looked away.

"How soon before the next one, do you think?" Emery asked as she glanced quickly toward the group of men in formal attire some distance away. The usual suspects were there: Caldwell, Pritchard, a few others, and Finnigan now returned.

Mary's shrewd brown eyes narrowed thoughtfully. "That probably bought her some time. Finnigan returned with his tail between his legs. The Gaggle undoubtedly senses your sister's mood this evening."

"And what mood is that?" I asked innocently.

"One that says you're not to be trifled with."

Mary was right. Ever since the encounter with Miles Griffin several weeks ago I'd felt more than the bland annoyance I always experienced at the attentions of

The Gaggle. I was bitter and angry that I'd been bested. Caught out. But there'd been something else. I was loath to call it disappointment, but that was the closest emotion I could name. I'd enjoyed my dance with the earl. And perhaps it was simply the idea of sharing time and space with someone who didn't know the truth of me. Honestly, I'd liked the way he looked at me, as more than a fortune to be won. He'd teased me, jested with me. No man ever did that.

I'd carefully cultivated a reputation since the death of my late husband. My goal was to appear a goddess on a pedestal too high to interact with mere mortal men. And these fortune hunters—these London dandies—believed it. They sought my favor with polite conversation. No one had dared to question the aura I projected. No one had figured out the truth.

I was just a woman, and a lonely one at that.

But Miles Griffin hadn't been fazed by my frosty exterior. He'd faced my wrath and countered with wry humor and blatant amusement. He'd cursed in my presence, for goodness' sake. It had been enough to surprise me and earn him a dance. A dance that had ended badly.

"Basilton is staring again," Emery reported.

I sighed. I didn't want his attention. I didn't know what to make of it. He'd yet to actually approach me. If he had some explanation—as Mary had asserted several times, much to my annoyance—then it was unknown to me. Basilton simply stared from his position in whatever room we happened to share.

"Ignore him," I advised. There was no point in considering the alternative, for I'd spent far too much time already considering his striking hazel eyes on me. I needed to stop replaying the waltz we'd shared and the small measure of freedom I'd experienced in his arms.

"Who are we ignoring?" came a voice behind us.

Mary, Emery, and I turned to see my brother-in-law, Augustus Ward, the Duke of Kendrick, press a soft kiss to my sister's temple.

"Are you done with your cigars and your brandy?" Emery inquired, her smile wide and pleased at her husband's appearance.

"I am. Good evening, ladies."

Mary and I returned his greeting, but Augustus was polite enough not to press the issue and repeat his earlier question.

"I thought I might collect my wife for a dance." Augie's blue eyes sparkled.

Something warm settled in my chest as I witnessed the scene. My happily married sister and her husband were fairly adorable. I didn't begrudge Emery her happiness in the least, but I couldn't fathom a marriage like hers. Mine had been so very different.

"I find that agreeable," Em responded before turning to me. "Dinner tomorrow? Mother and Father are arriving in the morning."

I nodded and smiled. "Of course. I will see you both then. Go enjoy your dance."

Augie whisked his bride away while Mary and I looked on.

"Are you ready to go, then?" my friend asked gently.

I wasn't sure how to answer that. I was done with this event but going home was a lonely prospect.

"Let's stay a little longer." I didn't know what I was waiting for, but when I cast a glance toward the column across the way, striking hazel eyes were no longer on me. Miles Griffin was gone.

Over the next hour, I declined four more dances—three from members of The Gaggle—and one with the elderly Marquess Stanton. Word was circulating that the widower was eager to secure wife number two in order to produce a male heir. He had three daughters older than my own eight and twenty.

I watched Mary—her red curls bouncing—glide in time with a reluctant Lord Pritchard, and smiled to myself. I'd begged off a dance with him, but my friend had smoothly stepped in and offered her services as a dance partner. Propriety and good breeding had earned his acceptance, and now Mary was moving elegantly about the floor with the unsmiling man. She was a good friend to know when I'd reached my limit. And Mary had her own reasons for interacting with my would-be suitors.

Glancing one last time to the empty pillar that Lord Basilton had been holding up most of the night, I let myself wonder—just for a moment—if he had anything to say for himself. Or if, like me, he'd gotten more than he'd bargained for with that unexpected dance.

I passed my shawl and reticule to Mr. Pitch in the grand foyer of Cawthorn Hall. I made for the stairs but winced.

"Are you well, Your Grace?" my butler asked kindly. He was forever checking on me.

I knew much of the staff pitied me. The young widow of that horrible duke. But I valued Mr. Pitch and his kindness. Perhaps because I'd been hardly older than a girl when I'd wed, several of the servants had seen fit to take extra care with me. I would repay their loyalty tenfold.

"Yes, Mr. Pitch. Just tender dancing feet." I smiled to reassure him.

I hadn't been lying to Thomas Faulk when I'd said these slippers were new and painful. Slipping off my slender heels, I thanked my butler before retreating to my quarters on the second floor.

The house was dark and quiet as I padded down the hallway. My steps and skirts seemed loud in the oppressive silence. The manor was too big and too empty. One would think I'd be used to it by now. And yet it was still preferable to the alternative.

I'd moved into Cawthorn Hall following my wedding to Albert Henney. During my first season at seventeen, as the daughter of a marquess, I'd made quite the match with the Duke of Cawthorn. Of course, he'd been many decades my senior. But after three marriages and becoming a widower that many times over, Cawthorn had been rather desperate for an heir. It turned out that even marrying a seventeen-year-old girl didn't ensure a fertile union. Pity that. If I'd at least been blessed with a child during our wretched five-year marriage, perhaps my life now wouldn't be so damnably quiet.

I'd just entered my bedchamber when Agatha, my lady's maid, entered my rooms and began lighting candles.

"Can I help you dress for bed, Your Grace?"

"Thank you, Agatha. I'd appreciate some help with this dress." It was a heavy, beaded monstrosity with an abundance of lace at the sleeves and hem and neckline as well.

Agatha was middle-aged and very kind. She'd been attending me since I left Hampshire and became duchess. Most of the staff had remained. I didn't require the dozens of servants that Albert had insisted upon, but I couldn't turn them out. Due to the marriage contract and stipulations therein, I had the funds to support their employ. And so they'd remained.

"How is your sister, Agatha?" I asked gently as she carefully undid the long row of buttons I couldn't reach.

"Oh, she's much improved, Your Grace. I received a letter just this morning. Her fever subsided and she's resting comfortably. Thank you for asking after her."

"Of course," I said, holding the bodice to me as it loosened and the weight of the dress pulled lower. "But if you need to travel to Dorset to attend to her or even just to pay her a visit, you are more than welcome to do so. Margaret can attend me in your absence, and I'm happy to pay the cost of your travels."

Agatha smiled indulgently at me. She wouldn't actually go. "Thank you, ma'am. You are very kind for offering."

I stepped out of my skirts and grabbed my dressing gown from the wardrobe as Agatha retrieved my dress and hung it up. "Just consider it." I smiled in her direction.

"I will, Your Grace. Will you be needing anything else? Mrs. Bunce made some shortbread cookies for the servants." Agatha lowered her voice before speaking again. "Would you like me to bring you a few?"

I laughed. It was kind of my maid to offer to pilfer treats from my cook. Mrs. Bunce was one of the only servants to prefer her life before the duke passed. I never figured out how Albert had gained the old woman's loyalty, but even now, nearly six years after his death, she hadn't taken to me. But I ate her mediocre meals and subsided on treats she made in secret for the servants. Little did she know, I had those in the household loyal to me as well.

"Thank you for thinking of me, but that won't be necessary. I'm quite tired. I think I shall go directly to bed. Good night, Agatha."

"Good night, Your Grace." And with that, she bobbed a curtsy and quietly closed the door behind her.

With a sigh, I settled at my dressing table and began the arduous task of removing pins from my elaborate coiffure. The room was warm, the abovestairs maid having lit and kept the fire going for my eventual return.

I hummed a little tune as my long hair unraveled and fell bit by bit down my back and over my shoulders. It felt good to free myself from the confines of the evening: my shoes that pinched, my dress that restrained, and the pins that so carefully held everything in place. I caught my reflection in the mirror and looked away. Time had a way of making its presence known, and I didn't always appreciate the reminder.

Discarding the sparkling tiara, I retrieved my hairbrush and began dragging the bristles through my pale blond locks. Thinking back on the events of the evening, I didn't know how much longer I could continue on attending society functions. The attention and the men were wearing me down. I grew more bitter and frustrated with every eager request to dance, all the disingenuous conversation, and the constant awareness of eyes upon me. I was exhausted.

The men in this town were relentless. I had to admit, I was surprised their efforts had gone on so long. I'd assumed they'd lose interest after my consistent refusals and unveiled disinterest. But no. Here we were. Over a year since I'd been overheard in a moment of frustration. I never should have made that declaration. Someone had overheard me vow to never marry again and word had spread far beyond what I'd intended.

I didn't understand what could possibly be holding the interest of these men, but I was nearing my breaking point. It was more than just The Gaggle. They were simply the most persistent in their efforts. But lords in every ballroom and parlor, at every luncheon or musicale, sought me out. Perhaps the amount of men in grievous debt far outnumbered the eligible ladies with dowries. I couldn't fathom the efforts these gentlemen went to in the attempt to secure my fortune.

Per the initial marriage agreement my father had made with Albert, I'd retained Cawthorn Hall—the duke's London residence—as well as his sizeable fortune following his death. The country seats and the title had passed to some distant relation. But the money and this home would be mine until I died. I supposed that was incentive enough for these men to pursue me doggedly. However, to me it seemed like more trouble than it was worth.

our very hallowed doorstep, I'd been summarily dismissed to the Continent to ensure my father's name and my courtesy title wouldn't be further besmirched.

And now I was back. Summoned through correspondence by the man opposite me.

"I have certain expectations for your return to London," he said. "You should focus your efforts this season on behavior befitting a man of your station as well as a member of this family. It is also time you consider taking a wife and producing an heir."

His stare was nothing short of expectant, so I nodded, assuming that was the correct response.

He resumed speaking, so I must have chosen wisely. "Any untoward action or degradation on your part would be most unfortunate and will not be tolerated if you'd like to remain on English soil."

"I see." I had no intention of going back to France, nor anywhere else. But I also didn't appreciate being dictated to.

Before my father could resume his sternly worded mandates, my mother breezed into the room.

"Oh, sorry to interrupt. Darling, there you are!"

I rose from my seat as Fiona Griffin, Marchioness Salisbury, placed a featherlight kiss to my cheek. She took the chair next to me and offered a bright smile.

"Hello, Mother," I greeted. We'd corresponded regularly during my exile. As complicated as my relationship was with the marquess, my mother loved and indulged me. It was her influence over my father that I'd miscalculated in the past. I'd assumed my doting mother could get me out of nearly anything, but apparently there was a limit to what my father would allow.

Looking back, I could see how much of an immature fool I'd been. And relying on the woman who loved me to clean up my messes wasn't a fair return on her devotion. I'd made a lot of mistakes back then. I didn't plan on taking my mother for granted any longer.

"How are you settling in? Do you need anything?"

"I am well, Mother. I assure you." I eyed the marquess, but decided it was better to bring up the lodging issue now rather than approaching my father later. The Basilton title came with both a yearly allowance and an estate. However, the estate was in Gloucester, with accompanying lands. I had no alternate residence here in London. "I've actually been making inquiries about townhomes available nearby." My parents shared a look I couldn't decipher. "I haven't been lucky in my acquisition just yet, but I'll be sure to keep you apprised of my plans."

My mother's lips pinched but she nodded quickly. I felt momentarily remorseful. She likely wanted me in residence. I'd been away for so long. But surely she could understand the need for my own space—my age and relationship with my father necessitated it.

Reaching over, I squeezed her hand gently. "But I promise to come around for dinner and tea whenever you like. You'll grow tired of my handsome face from seeing it so often."

Mother laughed as I intended.

Father's study descended into awkward silence.

After several beats, my mother smiled gamely and turned to me. "Well, Miles, why don't you join me for tea now? That's why I came to find you. And I trust your business with your father is quite settled, yes?"

I eyed the marquess warily, but his gaze remained steady and he made no move to interject. "Of course, Mother. I believe Father has said all he needs to say."

∽

Later that evening, I found myself at the club with the Marquess Daly and Augustus Ward, the Duke of Kendrick, of all people.

We were seated at a table in the main room and the atmosphere was quite rambunctious for a Thursday night.

Daly was sipping his Irish whiskey and playing host, smoothing any tension there was between myself and the duke. Truthfully, I was in good spirits despite the business with my father earlier in the day. And I had no qualms about sharing a drink with Kendrick. He, on the other hand, seemed to be reserving his judgment. Or perhaps he was simply reserved. I was fairly certain his suspicious and scrutinizing glances were due to his sister-in-law and what had transpired several weeks ago at the Hawkesberry ball.

"So what was your time like in France, Basil? You've yet to bring it up," Daly inquired easily.

"It was…" I let the statement hang momentarily while I refilled my glass. "Very French."

Daly barked a laugh. "Come now. That's all you have to say?"

It was my turn to laugh. There was no humor in it though. "I was forced from the country for being a naughty boy. Why would I want to talk about it?"

"It could not have truly been all bad."

It hadn't been. There had been entertainment to be had, new acquaintances, good food, and excellent wine. But it wasn't home. And to be honest, my pride had taken quite the hit upon my departure. It wasn't fresh but it was still there. An old wound. Scar tissue and a reminder of the reckless man I'd been.

Tracing the rim of the crystal, I finally managed, "It was not all bad."

A chorus of loud, inebriated laughter rang out to my left and I glared reflexively. I'd recently been avoiding these men in nearly every social situation. I didn't wish to become involved in their childish games. An association with them would be nothing more than a setback, as if six years hadn't gone by. As if I weren't someone new, remade from my experiences. I wanted to be a man who learned from his past as well as his mistakes. And there was no future in resuming my friendships with any of the men at that table. I'd grown and changed. They'd clung to their circumstances and eschewed everything else.

"Were we ever quite so annoying?" Daly asked as he too made note of the rowdy group beside us.

Risking a glance, I took in the drunken, jovial men. Thomas Faulk, Ebenezer Petty, Pritchard, and Simon Edgemoore. The very same men who'd welcomed me to London and had damned me all the same.

"I certainly never was," Kendrick said from his place across from me. I thought he might be telling the truth.

"Nor I," I claimed with a smirk.

Daly laughed. "That's not true at all, Basil. But my memory is fading in my old age, so I'll let it stand."

I smiled ruefully, wishing he wasn't right.

With an assessing gaze, Kendrick wondered aloud, "You don't wish to join them this evening, Basilton?"

I glanced up sharply. "Perhaps at one time. But no longer." And it was the truth. I regretted my perceived association with the men at the next table. They'd ruined…whatever that had been with the Duchess of Cawthorn. Or maybe I had ruined it and needed someone to blame.

I thought back to her angry, betrayed expression and stifled a wince.

Seeing her in recent weeks hadn't diminished her appeal. Patricia Henney was loveliness personified, her appearance always impeccable and her bearing consistently aloof. She was still hidden behind her frozen walls. But I'd seen—and heard—the truth of her, for just a few moments on that balcony. There was more to her than that untouchable, ruthless woman, and I wanted to know her. I couldn't explain it and I didn't know why, but I'd felt it when we'd danced. A connection. A thread tying me to her. I needed to see if the line went both ways.

I hadn't approached her yet. I valued my life, after all, and she didn't appear the forgiving sort. But I hadn't given up hope just yet. If I could just get her alone to talk, explain myself. Perhaps she'd see reason. But she was always with someone. When our eyes did happen to meet, I could feel her walls slamming into place, freezing me out before I even managed the wherewithal to approach.

Perhaps the first step to gaining the duchess's trust was happening here and now. I knew who Kendrick was to her. Winning his favor—hell, simply his understanding—might go a long way if I ever hoped to speak to Patricia Henney again.

Taking but a moment to consider, I settled easily on honesty and offered without prompting, "I didn't know who the duchess was when we danced. On my honor. It was not my intention to deceive her or become involved in some nefarious plot."

Kendrick's gaze was assessing. "Patty has been through a great deal. I've known her, in some capacity, my whole life. My wife would sink rabid claws into you if you even thought about hurting her sister. And that doesn't even account for what Patty herself would do to you. So it is with utmost sincerity that I advise you to proceed with caution."

I met Kendrick's eyes and hoped he could read the earnestness there. "I will heed your warning and offer gratitude for your advice, Your Grace."

"Ho! Basil!" shouted Thomas Faulk as if suddenly noticing my presence not ten feet away. "Come have a drink with us!"

Kendrick's eyes had not left mine, so I could see the curiosity along with the challenge.

With a nod, I turned to the group at the next table and said, "Good evening, Finnigan. I appreciate your offer but I find myself inclined to stay right here."

A few of the men laughed but Lord Finnigan simply appeared confused and very much in his cups. I didn't wait for his brain to catch up with his ears and simply returned my attention to Daly and Kendrick.

After a moment, Augustus picked up his—mostly full—glass and toasted mine where it sat. "Cheers," he said and took a swallow. I did the same, feeling like I'd passed a test. Or, at the very least, that the duke was giving me the benefit of the doubt rather than a ringing endorsement. "Well, Basilton, are you coming to the Westbrooke ball tomorrow?"

Briefly considering the invitations my mother had stacked neatly in my study, I nodded thoughtfully. "I believe so."

"Good," said Kendrick. "I think that would be a wise decision."

I raised my brows in response. Perhaps the ringing endorsement wasn't as far off as I assumed. Would the Duchess of Cawthorn be in attendance, I wondered?

"Well, I will be there as well, in case anyone was curious," Daly said with an aggrieved pout.

"Yes. Yes. We know. You attend every event. Are you finally on the hunt for a wife, Daly?" I asked with a smirk. I knew he wasn't. The Marquess Daly had a mistress. The very same mistress he'd had before I went to the Continent. I feared my friend was doomed to love a woman he could never marry, someone so far outside the aristocracy that even his reputation wouldn't allow it.

"Perhaps I am," he countered, followed by another swig of whiskey.

Kendrick's eyes met mine and our surprised brows rose in unison.

"Perhaps I am," he repeated, softer and slower, before closing his eyes.

I snatched his glass before he could set it on the edge of the table. "How much of that bottle did you have?"

"Enough," Daly said without opening his eyes, "to make me maudlin."

Kendrick shook his head. "Come on, man. Time to go."

Between the two of us, the duke and I managed to lead Daly out of the club and into Kendrick's conveyance.

"I'll see him home," Kendrick assured me, foot resting on the step of the carriage. "I don't believe he planned on that level of intoxication, nor that amount of honesty."

"I'm sure he will come to regret both in the light of day," I said with a laugh.

"I hope you don't regret your honesty this evening," Kendrick said earnestly, no threat in his tone.

Voice even, I replied, "I meant what I said."

"Good," Augustus said with a quick grin. With a firm slap to my shoulder, he rose up into the carriage and called out, "See you tomorrow at Westbrooke's. Make it count."

I watched the well-appointed carriage trundle down the lane and out of sight, thinking I might have just been given some support in my efforts with the duchess. I would not waste the opportunity.

Perhaps tomorrow I could see if that enigmatic thread between us was still present, and give it a little tug.

Four

PATTY

With careful steps, I descended the carriage into the soggy autumn morning. I pulled my cloak tighter around my shoulders and steeled myself for the day to come.

With a quiet "Thank you" for my footman, I bustled determinedly up the steps to the orphanage in the East End.

The administrator and I were on friendly terms. Mrs. Watford greeted me with a warm smile in the foyer of the great hall. The building had seen some significant renovation over the years. It was no longer drafty and cold on the interior, and the space beyond was large enough to house the children who lived here comfortably. No more sharing of beds and eating and living on top of one another.

"Welcome, Your Grace," the middle-aged woman said happily as she reached for my cloak. "Here, let me take that."

"Thank you, Mrs. Watford. How do you do?"

"I'm well, ma'am. Shall we take tea in my office before you visit the children?" Carefully folding my dark cloak over her arm, the woman regarded me with bright eyes the color of amber.

"That sounds lovely," I agreed, following the headmistress and my cloak.

We reached a well-lit study, and Mrs. Watford hung my items just inside the door before offering me a seat near the fireplace. I noticed plenty of fuel nearby for burning, money having been put to good use. Rather than assuming a position of power behind her desk, Mrs. Watford joined me in the matching armchair after instructing a young maid to return with tea.

And as always, once the plump older woman was settled, she dove right in with updates and improvements. "You'll be happy to hear that three of the older children have been placed as apprentices with good masters. And the repairs on the second-floor dormitory are finally complete. Your most recent donation of books was very well received and some of the children asked if Saint Nicolas had visited early."

"That is wonderful news," I interjected before she could rattle off any more information to validate my giving. I didn't come here to ensure my philanthropy was warranted or well-earned. I came here for the children. And if I didn't stop Mrs. Watford's helpful recitation, she'd continue all morning.

She meant well, I knew that. But I didn't need her constant justification for my time and funds. I'd appointed her the person in charge. I'd researched what was required and interviewed countless individuals. She had been the very best person for the position, and I trusted her to do her job. Mrs. Watford was long past needing to prove herself to me. Yet she refused to accept that.

Tea arrived and she busied herself with that momentarily, so I continued, "The children should be preparing for their midmorning break shortly, is that correct?" I knew the education schedule, but it felt prudent to confirm.

"Oh, yes." She glanced to the timepiece on the mantel. "In just about a quarter hour."

"Perfect," I said, smiling.

"You know you're welcome to interrupt their lessons. You needn't coordinate your visits around our schedule, Your Grace."

I swallowed uncomfortably. I didn't want my presence here to be a disruption for the children or their caretakers and instructors. My goal was to make their lives better, and consistency and stability went a long way for these children. Realistically, I knew an innocent visit would not impact their daily instruction too terribly much, but I felt it was important that they saw me abiding by rules and common courtesy. Disrespecting their obligations and responsibilities would set the wrong precedent, I feared. So I planned my visits accordingly.

"Thank you, Mrs. Watford. But I'm happy to make myself available at times convenient for you and your staff."

She smiled and resumed her superfluous reporting on improvements made in the month prior, and described the addition of two new children to Watford House. I sighed inwardly and drank my tea, counting down the minutes until I could see the children.

~

"D-d-do you like my drawing, Your Grace?"

I smiled at the angelic little face, and said with much enthusiasm, "Yes, Francesca. I think that is the finest picture of a butterfly I've ever seen."

I'd been mobbed in the main hall when the children entered for their midmorning break for tea, a snack, and a short recreational period. After I'd greeted all thirty-eight children—including the two new additions from Covent Garden—they'd all finally settled down. I'd circulated and joined small clusters of children and asked after their studies and their health. Most had been in exceedingly good spirits and thrilled at the prospect of having a visitor.

Francesca, who loved to draw, had let her tea go cold while she focused her efforts. She had managed the tea cakes though. I smiled at the thought. I'd eventually settled down beside her on the bench, stuffing my modest skirts beneath the table. The young girl's stammer was much improved. The nurses on staff here at Watford House had assured me years ago that Francesca's stutter was developmental in nature and would likely abandon her as she aged.

The nearly six-year-old beamed at my effusive praise, and resumed her charcoal sketch of a garden, tongue poking out in concentration.

I'd taken to the girl early on in our acquaintance. Years ago, before the orphanage was Watford House, I'd visited the previous establishment with my friend Mary Lovelace. We'd toured the facility in a fit of despair on Mary's part. She had been—and still was—desperate for a child. Her extreme nature had led her to the steps of the orphanage with a singular goal in mind. I'd accompanied her because she was my dearest friend, and the situation called for support.

Upon viewing the poor conditions of the orphanage and the children within, we'd been overwhelmed. Mary had fought tears and rage throughout the visit and had collapsed in a heartbroken heap on the carriage ride back to Mayfair. Her guilt at being unable to help all the children in need had broken something within. She'd abandoned her schemes and unconventional methods for obtaining a family on her own that very day.

I'd been similarly afflicted by the conditions I'd witnessed. My heart had squeezed painfully to see the unwashed, crying children. The plight of the overworked staff and nursemaids was troubling, to say the least. Mary had found our visit too painful to contemplate and never wished to repeat it again.

My resolve had taken a different form. I'd been determined to see change enacted, so I'd taken my ill-gotten monetary gains and put them to good use. I took over the orphanage and kept everyone on staff who wished to remain. Hiring thirty percent more employees helped lighten the load they all carried. And installing Mrs. Watford as the new figurehead and namesake ensured that my expectations for the facility would be met, as well as diverted attention from myself as owner of the establishment.

Now the children were clean and healthy. They received age-appropriate education from governesses and tutors I'd interviewed along with Mrs. Watford. And when they reached adolescence, the administration worked diligently to find apprenticeships and positions with reputable tradesmen and households in London.

Now, six years later, my plans for Watford House had been fully realized. This was tangible change. Visible proof of the good I could do with the Cawthorn funds. My marriage hadn't been in vain after all. I was proud of the work I'd done here, and visiting Francesca and the other children was the best part of my day.

I watched as the tiny artist's hand left a charcoal smudge across the bridge of her nose. Taking a handkerchief out of my reticule, I quickly swiped at the offending mark. Francesca giggled and rubbed her nose again, leaving an even bigger smear. I laughed as she resumed her task under my watchful gaze.

As my plans for the orphanage had taken shape and the roots had buried themselves in fresh soil, I'd realized the difference I could make in a single child's life. Providing safety and a future for them made me long for security and a family. And that was why I'd never confessed to Mary—nor anyone else—my involvement with Watford House. My friend was so eager for a family that at one time she'd been reckless enough to decide to eschew society's mandates and acquire one on her own, regardless of her family's inevitable disapproval and her place in society. But after that awful day and the terrible things she'd witnessed, she'd never spoken of visiting an orphanage again. I didn't think Mary had been prepared for the realities she'd faced then, so much so that even the horrifying prospect of finding a husband in Mayfair seemed the more suitable route to take.

"Children!" called one of the instructors before meeting my eyes. "It's time to say goodbye to the duchess and return to your studies."

A chorus of goodbyes rang out as they stood from the communal tables in the hall and followed their teachers back to their schoolrooms.

Francesca reached over for a quick embrace and my throat tightened as I said goodbye to the little girl with pretty dark brown curls and lovely hazel eyes.

"This is f-f-for you," she said, handing me her drawing.

I swallowed against the emotion pressing insistently on my airway, and smiled. "Thank you, Francesca. I shall treasure it always."

She smiled and took off running, charcoal in hand.

I sat there for long moments, rubbing my fingers over the dark smudge of coal dust on the fabric of my emerald skirts. Eventually a maid entered to clean up the remnants of tea and cakes left behind, so I went in search of my wrap.

Carefully rolling up Francesca's drawing, I tucked it against the cloak's fabric lining and made my way back out into the soggy autumn day, bound for Cawthorn Hall, alone once more.

"He's watching you again," Emery whispered behind her fan, blond head tilted in my direction.

Later that evening, I was once again positioned between my sister, Emery, and my friend, Mary. We were at the Westbrooke ball and it was an absolute crush. There were so many people around that the ballroom was stifling and we were barely conversing at the risk of being overheard by gossipy eavesdroppers.

My gaze followed Emery's to the three men positioned near an open window. Damn them for having the foresight to claim even the off chance of a cooling breeze.

The smells of candle wax and fresh flowers were overwhelming. I fluttered my fan and leaned toward my sister's ear, murmuring, "It looks like you are being watched as well."

I saw the corners of her mouth lift and wondered what my brother-in-law was playing at. Augustus was ensconced near the window with Miles Griffin, consummate lurker, and the Marquess Daly—well known to us now due to his friendship with Augie. All three men looked in our direction before turning back to their small, masculine circle.

"I can't hear anything over here," Mary whined. "What's going on?"

I leaned away from Emery and toward my friend. "We are wondering what Augie and Daly and Basilton are all doing over there watching us."

Mary's wild red curls brushed close by as she tilted her head to see around all the bodies in the room in the direction we'd indicated. "Whoops, apologies. You know my hair does what it wants."

I smiled. "Much like its owner."

Mary beamed. "Exactly." But then she grew serious. "Do you really think Augustus would be conversing with Basilton if the man was truly devious like all the others?"

I frowned, unused to considering the motivations of men. Did I trust Augie's judgment? I honestly did. He was my sister's husband and I'd known him my whole life. The Duke of Kendrick was one of the best men I knew, and that list was exceedingly short.

However, I didn't trust Miles Griffin. And I didn't know the circumstances under which he'd approached Augie. Perhaps my brother-in-law was too polite to cause a scene in this ballroom. The Earl of Basilton could be attempting to court my favor by appealing to Augustus. That would be a waste. Augie would see right through him, if that was the case.

Still, it was curious, this arrangement of gentlemen.

Moments later, Daly broke away from his comrades. He made his way through the crowd with ease, offering polite nods as he advanced until he was standing right before me.

"Your Grace, good evening."

"Hello, Daly. Having fun?"

He smiled. "I am now." Any flirtation with the marquess was harmless. Everyone knew he was in love with his longtime mistress. He posed no threat to me, with neither unwanted attentions nor intent.

With a short bow, he turned to my companions. "Lady Mary. Duchess. I hope you're both enjoying the festivities."

"What's going on over there, Daly?" Emery asked, indicating her husband and Miles Griffin.

"Oh, just two gentlemen getting acquainted." Emery looked like she wanted to say more but Daly turned to me and asked, "Your Grace, might I sign your dance card this evening?"

I looked up, somewhat surprised. We'd danced before, the marquess and I, but not often. As I said, there was no risk involved. Daly wasn't after my hand nor my ample purse. But on the way to their target, my eyes snagged on Basilton across the way. He was watching our exchange attentively. I didn't know if some odd male posturing was in progress, but I didn't see the harm in dancing with Daly at some point this evening.

"Of course," I answered easily after but a moment's hesitation. As I held up my wrist, Daly retrieved my dance card and scratched quickly across the surface.

I lowered my hand to my side as he said, "I chose the next waltz." I nodded. "But for now, I'm off for some refreshment. Would you ladies care for anything?"

Mary answered in the affirmative and Daly was off, winding his way again through the crush.

That was…odd.

Shrugging off the sensation that Daly was behaving strangely, I glanced over to where Miles Griffin was conversing with Augustus. But both men were on the move toward us. I noticed distractedly that the previous quadrille was close to ending, and wondered why Daly would have requested a dance and then bolted away for refreshment.

The gentlemen reached us and offered polite greetings. Augustus introduced the man at his side to Emery and Mary, while I looked on suspiciously. However, I responded appropriately while I fought to keep the unease off my face.

The Earl of Basilton smiled, hardly glancing at my companions. "I've come to claim my dance, Duchess. I believe the waltz is due any moment."

I smiled, all teeth. "Apologies, my lord. But that dance has already been claimed."

With a meaningful glance to the card about my wrist, he replied, "Oh, I'm aware."

My smile slipped off my face as I turned the dance card over and read quite plainly the masculine scrawl accompanying the next waltz: *Miles Griffin, Earl of Basilton.*

Gaze narrowed, I looked to Augie, for he had been part of this…this…deception. He met my stare unflinchingly, and to my great confusion gave me a small wink. What was he playing at? And why was he obviously helping Basilton?

Heads nearby were turning in our direction. The music had finally stopped as the quartet prepared for the next set.

I felt quite certain that Miles Griffin would cause a scene, if need be, to claim this duplicitous dance. And I, Patricia Henney, did not entertain fodder for *ton* gossip.

A cold mask of indifference solidified on my features as I returned my wrist to my side. "It seems, Lord Basilton, that the next dance is yours."

"Oh, hell," Mary breathed next to me, barely audible.

Basilton beamed and held out his hand. I took it and did my best to crush every bone in his smug appendage.

With a surprised squeak, he extracted his limb and turned my hand to tuck it into his elbow upon his well-tailored black jacket. I fought a laugh at his inadvertent sound.

Without breaking stride he led us to the dance floor, unperturbed.

"If I pinch the inside of your elbow, will you make that high-pitched squawk again?" I asked sweetly.

"It was a manly squawk, actually. And no, I will not. For I am now prepared for your brand of revenge. Violent thing, aren't you?"

Moving us into position at the edge of the dance floor, he seemed to notice the blasted Gaggle at the same time I did. With a quietly uttered curse, he escorted me toward the center of the floor instead.

Facing him, I awaited the musicians to signal the start of the dance. The earl and I watched each other, victorious and vengeful smiles having faded to something…else. His brilliant eyes regarded me, and I knew I was just as expectant in my own gaze.

Finally the first strains of the violin emerged and we moved in time with the other dancers.

Basilton took the opportunity to whisper, "I'm sorry for using Daly to trick you into something. It wasn't nefarious or malicious. I simply needed to speak to you."

I frowned. The irritation at being fooled lingered, making my words sharper than I intended. "Why didn't you just approach me? I've seen you at half a dozen events in the last fortnight."

He stepped close, hand light upon my waist as we circled. The barely there reminder of his nearness was distracting. Finally, he said, "I wanted to speak to you alone. And you were always surrounded. I didn't think your friends would appreciate my intrusion."

Muscle memory guided my steps as I focused my attention on my dance partner. I feared I was overly attentive as I took in his earnest expression. I could discern every color that made up his brilliant eyes. Mossy green tonight, with striations of gold.

Swallowing, I forced myself to look away from his hypnotic gaze. *What is the matter with me?*

"What are you going to do?" Mary asked.

I cast her a curious glance. "What do you mean?"

"Patty," was her flat response.

I widened my eyes. "What?"

"He's outrageously handsome. And I know you find him so. I also know that no other man has ever made you…like this."

"Like what?" I demanded. "And don't say squishy."

Mary huffed a laugh. "That's just it, Patty. No other man has ever made you… anything. He's turned your head and caught your attention. There is no precedent for this."

I took a bracing breath because she was right. "Well, I haven't determined if that is a good or a bad thing."

With a quick glance for anyone who might have wandered nearby, Mary finally lowered her voice and said what she'd clearly been waiting all night to say. "I think you should take him as a lover."

My eyes shot to hers. This was bold, even for the outrageous Mary Lovelace.

She rolled her eyes. "Just consider it for a moment. You've never been interested in men as anything more than unfortunate fixtures in society, best to be avoided at all costs. Your husband was a monster. But, Patty, not all men are that way. Some are worthless and troublesome, yes. But Basilton has piqued your interest, and I don't think you should ignore that. It's revolutionary that for the first time in your life, you've noticed a man—as a woman, with wants and needs and desires. Perhaps there is some healing that could come of this. You could take what you want, on your own terms. And I think you would be safe with the earl. He doesn't seem to take anything too seriously, so you wouldn't have to worry about an attachment. You could be up front with him and tell him exactly what you want."

I considered Patty's words as she spoke, uncomfortable with the attention and the references to my horrible marriage and the deficiencies of my character. "I'm not broken, Mary."

The hand not holding her lemonade grabbed my own, demanding my attention. "Hush. Of course you're not. That's not what I'm saying. Anyone who went through what you did at the hands of the duke would have scars. That doesn't make you less. It has simply made you cautious. And there is nothing wrong with that. I just want you to be happy."

Clearing my throat, I attempted to banish the emotion rising as well. "And you think Basilton could make me happy?" I'd meant for the question to sound preposterous, but it came out quiet and curious instead.

Mary squeezed my hand. "Maybe," she admitted. "If nothing else, he looks like he knows his way around a four-poster. So you could at least have some fun."

Five

MILES

"What is the matter, darling?"

Drawn by my mother's words, I blinked away from the paper in my hand. Another letter, totaling nine rejections and missed opportunities.

With a smile that likely still clung to my confused frustration, I met her expectant gaze over a breakfast table laden with more than was strictly necessary. "Nothing, Mother. It seems another property in town has eluded me. I had hoped that nearly a month of searching and viewing residences would yield some positive results."

Mother looked away and fiddled with her teacup and saucer. "Yes, well. I'm sure it's just a busy time with families and gentlemen seeking accommodations for the season."

She didn't meet my eyes as she said any of this, and an odd pressure settled into the dining room where we were eating alone. My father had an early speaking engagement this morning, and I was somewhat relieved by his resulting absence. Our interactions remained strained and tense, though few and far between they might be.

Despite my frustrating lack of accommodations, it was not my intent to make my mother unhappy about my impending departure from our family home.

It was obvious that my arrival for the season was on the tips of their tongues. Fielding their curious glances and baiting for more information about my return, I diverted every conversation into a charm offensive to distract nosy matrons and the like.

After half an hour I was exhausted from diversion and expectations. Attempting to be a respectable gentleman felt like a lot of work. In my youthful days, I'd simply said and done whatever outrageous things had suited my mood. And if word of my antics spread to the Marquess Salisbury, then all the better.

Now that I had the attention of what seemed like everyone in the *ton*, all I wanted was to be myself, which was frightfully boring and sedate these days. Past Miles would have been jubilant with the attention for it would have been an opportunity to rebel.

"I see the Fenwicks," Mother said quietly, adjusting her feathered cap. "I wish to speak with them. You go on ahead. I'm sure some of your acquaintances are here. I'll catch up shortly."

"As you wish, Mother."

She broke away from me in one smooth movement, and I took a deep breath. I continued my measured pace along the path, intent on locating a secluded bench to hide and wait for her return.

"Ho, Basil!"

The shouted exclamation turned my head as well as a few others. Pivoting and seeing the owner of the conspicuous voice nearly made me roll my eyes at his sudden inability to be discreet. Approaching me from behind was Mr. George Shepard, an editor at the *London Post*.

With a sly glance for any eavesdroppers, I greeted my companion as he fell in step beside me. "Mr. Shepard. How do you do?"

"I'm well, Basil. I was happy to hear you were back in London." His sincerity was unmistakable.

The gentleman at my side had always been a true friend. Several years my senior, George and I had been acquainted for some time. Before my exile, he'd been printing stories about my sainted father for years. Until he'd been gifted an article that was less than flattering to the Marquess Salisbury.

I slowed my steps and allowed several ladies to pass us by before speaking in a low voice, "Thank you, George. I'm happy to be back."

Concern bled through his tone when he spoke next. "I wanted to see you. But wasn't sure if I should call on you. I know I said so in my letters, but, Bas, I'm so sorry that things worked out the way they did with the article. If I had known—"

"No," I interrupted before he could place the blame on himself. "It wasn't your fault. I knew the risk involved. I was arrogant, and thought myself invincible. You tried to warn me." I brought us to a stop and turned to my longtime friend, making my expression earnest and forthright. "I don't blame you for how things turned out. I truly do not. I earned my time in France all on my own."

George didn't seem convinced. His gray eyes were troubled as he watched me.

"All is well," I assured him with a genuine smile. "Now, tell me of yourself. We've exchanged a handful of letters over the years, but I'm eager to hear how you're getting on."

My friend slowly relaxed as he discussed his family and his success at the newspaper. We chatted amiably for some time. Finally, George admitted he needed to drop by his office on Fleet Street to follow up on a few things before the next issue went to print. "But let's have a drink soon, Basil. It's damn good to see you."

I agreed easily. No matter how complicated our past, George Shepard was a good friend, and I was happy to see him again.

After he went on his way, I continued walking in the other direction. My mother was still preoccupied somewhere behind me. I spied Augustus Ward, the Duke of Kendrick, in conversation with someone up ahead off the path. The other man looked vaguely familiar but I couldn't place him. The two gentlemen were conversing in the grass beneath a large shade tree still clinging to gold and orange leaves. Two horses were waiting nearby.

Kendrick caught sight of me and waved me over. With a wry tip of my hat, I joined the men.

"Basilton," the duke greeted with a small twist of his lips.

"Good day, gentlemen," I returned.

"Silas, this is Miles Griffin, the Earl of Basilton." Kendrick indicated the tall gentleman with a tilt of his head. "And, Basilton, this is Silas Bartholomew, son of the Marquess Northcutt and my brother-in-law," he finished pointedly.

Ah, so this was the Duchess of Cawthorn's elder brother, hence the familiarity.

We shook hands, and Bartholomew appeared jovial by all accounts. Perhaps he didn't know about the business between Patricia and myself.

"So, you're the one who tricked not one but two dances out of Patty," he said with a beaming smile.

So much for that thought.

I huffed a laugh and looked down momentarily. "Yes, well. I see my reputation precedes me. Some things never change," I added belatedly, bitterness hovering at the edge of my tone. The morning was clearly taking its toll on me.

"Oh, come now, Basilton. I'm just having a lark. It is so rare that anyone gets anything over on my sister—any of them—that it must be noted. Unless it's me." He laughed. "I best them regularly."

I took in his still smiling face, remembering belatedly that Silas Bartholomew was behind me at university. Yet his dark brown hair was graying at the temples, so he appeared older and more distinguished. I felt like a bit of a ruffian in his presence with my longer hair swept underneath my hat, despite being his elder.

"I don't believe for one second that I bested the duchess in anything. I merely made myself…memorable."

Brown eyes sparkling, Bartholomew nodded agreeably. "You might be right. Perhaps gaining Patty's notice is the best one could hope for."

I considered his words and how the duchess presented herself for the world to see. And then I remembered the hunch of her slim shoulders and the quietly uttered curse that had necessitated her escape from the ballroom on the night we met.

Perhaps I wanted to gain more than Patricia's notice.

In an attempt at levity, I returned, "Well, with any luck we've reached a peaceful state and she no longer wishes for my immediate demise. Although I don't imagine we'll be dancing anytime soon. I don't want to push my luck."

Kendrick snorted. "That's probably a wise decision."

Bartholomew's smile stayed firmly in place but his eyes lost some of their amusement. "Perhaps that is sensible," he agreed. "She's been through quite a lot, my sister."

I nodded, but glanced to Kendrick. His expression was closed and it was obvious that no further information would be forthcoming on whatever made Silas Bartholomew suddenly protective of his sister. I didn't really know the circumstances surrounding her marriage beyond the fact that the Duke of Cawthorn had been in his eighties when he'd died years ago, with no heir. All gossip on the subject was likely too old to still be circulating.

She would have been a terribly young bride. The thought had uneasiness settling in my gut. Had her marriage been awful? Was that what made these gentlemen appear both sad and defensive when speaking about her?

They were her family. Surely they had the right to worry. But something about the thinly veiled pity radiating from them didn't sit right. Not for one such as the duchess.

"And yet," I said enigmatically.

Silas Bartholomew raised a brow. "And yet?"

"She is a force to be reckoned with," I challenged.

Kendrick wore a small, approving smile. And Bartholomew's expression sobered as he considered me, and then quite without warning a smile exploded across his features.

"Oh, Augie. You were right." I looked between the men, alarmed. "Basilton," Silas continued, unperturbed, "you poor idiot."

Frowning, I asked, "What do you mean?"

Bartholomew sighed happily and ignored me completely. "I never thought I'd say this, but I'm exceedingly glad I came back to London this season."

My cheeks felt inexplicably warm as I stared at the two men who suddenly seemed more like gossipy chits than anything else. Before I could question their assumptions, Silas spoke once more.

Six

PATTY

Miles Griffin was in my sister's drawing room when I arrived. He was sipping whiskey or brandy or some other such beverage while speaking happily to my brother. His dark trousers and jacket hugged his tall form. The blue-patterned waistcoat he wore accentuated his trim waist. And the dark hair brushed casually away from his face landed just below his ears. I felt the sudden urge to run my fingers through the nearly black locks before behaving like a two-year-old and twisting it violently.

What in the bloody hell was Lord Basilton doing at a family dinner party?

Basilton looked up then, as if sensing the heat of my frustration. He paused in conversation with Silas and offered me an unbothered, blinding smile—straight white teeth on full display, and God help me, a dimple in his right cheek.

My interfering brother turned, following the earl's gaze. "Patty! Get over here. You're just in time."

I remained frozen near the threshold of the drawing room despite Silas's urging and took in the remaining occupants of the room. Augustus and Mary were chatting near the fireplace, both of them having noted my appearance in the doorway. Augie looked cautious—smart man. Mary appeared positively gleeful, which was as good as confirmation that something was afoot.

I raised an imperious eyebrow at my friend's gloating smile before turning back to regard Basilton. My brother had returned to his animated method of storytelling and Miles was mostly paying attention in between sneaking amused glances at me.

Then I nearly jumped out of my slippers when Emery murmured from directly beside my ear, "Now you're the one staring."

"Emery," I hissed in exasperation. "Good lord, you need a bell or louder underskirts."

She smiled indulgently before handing me a glass of wine. "I wasn't being intentionally sneaky, sister. But you did seem rather preoccupied."

I glared. "What is he doing here?"

"Silas invited him. They met in the park yesterday and are apparently now good friends."

Scowling, I glanced back to the man in question. Augustus and Mary had joined my brother and Basilton. The foursome seemed suspiciously cheerful.

My little sister's warm hand on my arm pulled my attention away from the other side of the drawing room. Concerned amber eyes looked up at me. "Is this all right, Patty? I don't want you to be uncomfortable. And I thought you and the earl had made amends somewhat."

"We've reached a potential understanding," I confirmed.

Emery hadn't removed her hand from the ice-blue fabric covering my arm. "I'll ask him to leave if you wish. I wanted you to have a night to relax in our company. You're so constantly on guard at society events. I thought a nice dinner among friends and family would be a welcome respite."

I sighed and felt the tightness of my features loosen. "I appreciate the effort, Emery. I do. But I am fine, I assure you."

Emery continued as if I hadn't responded, "You're under so much pressure, and constantly bombarded with attention from all those would-be suitors. It must be suffocating. I want you to feel like, here and now, you can take a deep breath and just…be yourself for a night."

Finally smiling at the care and concern from my protective sister, I admitted, "You do not need to ask him to leave. I do feel comfortable in your home, Em. And Basilton's presence here will not change that." The man had seen more sides to me than I cared to consider, and none of them were the daunting duchess facade I typically wore for my peers. He'd witnessed my frustration and vulnerability. He'd even provoked my ire so entirely that I'd threatened bodily harm in public. That said more about me than it did about him unfortunately.

And perhaps I was a little bit embarrassed when I thought about our interactions. He felt familiar in a way that put me on edge.

It was easier to live a lie when no one saw the truth. And Miles Griffin had witnessed more truths in our short acquaintance than I was comfortable with.

"You're sure?" Emery sought to confirm.

Clearing away my confusing thoughts, I offered a genuine smile. "I am."

After a protracted moment where Emery sought to discern the veracity of my statement by utilizing severe eye contact and mind reading, she finally turned to the room and announced that dinner was ready to be served.

Augustus moved forward to escort my sister into the dining room. He passed me with a quiet, "All right, Patty?"

But before I could answer in the affirmative, my idiot brother bounded forward and tucked my arm through his. "Lead the way, Patty. I'm famished. You'll need to support me to the dining table in my weakened state."

"You're ridiculous," I accused, a reluctant smile tugging the corners of my lips.

I had missed Silas. Though I'd never admit it to his handsome face. He was an extravagant personality and had entertained everyone in his orbit for his entire life. He sought to keep the peace and put people at ease with humor and self-deprecation. My brother exasperated my mother with his outlandish behavior and his constant avoidance of the London season and potential brides. But Silas could drag a smile out of anyone. He'd been in and out of London for much of my time there, but he always visited during his stays in town. I'd seen more of Silas since my marriage to Albert than anyone else in my family. But this was the longest he intended to remain in town in recent memory. Mama was thrilled and assumed he'd decided to find a wife. I wasn't so sure what Silas's motivation

I didn't need to wait long.

"I think you should take Basilton as a lover," Mary said proudly.

Emery's fingers stilled on her skirts.

"I know how you feel, Mary. You've mentioned this already," I replied evenly, neither censure nor surprise in my tone.

"And you discounted my genius idea in favor of ignoring him and acting odd all through dinner."

I rolled my eyes. "I was not behaving strangely. I was merely unhappy being viewed as a zoo animal on display for your nefarious machinations."

It was Mary's turn to roll her eyes. "Come now. I had nothing to do with Basilton being here this evening. I'm sorry for staring, but the two of you *were* putting on a show. It was entertaining to watch."

I scoffed. Emery remained silent, eyes wide and watchful.

"What?" Mary asked. "It was a revelation to see you like that with a man. Engaged and amused…and…and *yourself*. You looked happy, Patty. And I was happy to see you happy. Weren't you happy to see your sister happy, Emery?"

Emery did not take the bait. No matter, because Mary continued on, unaffected.

"It wasn't malicious. How could you think that?" Her tone had finally gone serious, abandoning her jesting. "I want, more than anything, for you to be happy. And I'm not saying you need to marry Miles Griffin. But there is obviously something between the two of you. Perhaps you could enjoy each other's company."

"You overstep. And presume too much," I said haughtily.

"Oh come off it. Don't act like we're all delicate flowers here. Your sister is too polite to say it, but she agrees with me."

I looked to Emery who swallowed uneasily. "I'm sorry if Basilton's presence made you feel cornered or conspired against, Patty. That was not our intent." She cast a quick glance to Mary who looked disappointed. "I think I'm going to retire. You ladies stay as long as you'd like."

Emery left amid my protests and reassurances. Mary remained quiet and watchful. Once my sister had exited, I rounded on my friend. "See what you did? Don't try to use Emery for your own ends. She's not comfortable with that."

"Because she's still unsure with you, Patty. She's still afraid one small misstep will drive you out of her life again. She's too afraid to tell you the truth about Basilton or anything else that might cause you any upset."

My nose burned and emotion clogged my throat. "That's not fair," I choked.

Emery and I had found our way back to one another. After I'd married the Duke of Cawthorn at seventeen, I'd remained trapped in London in my unhappy marriage. My sister was never one for city life and our meetings were very few over the years. I knew Emery had resented the person I'd become in order to have a successful season and land a titled husband. I didn't blame her. I'd hated who I'd become as well.

Even after Albert's death, I'd remained in London to see through my work at Watford House. And to be honest, the thought of spending time in Hampshire—in our family home—did nothing but fill me with dread. It was a reminder of the bright-eyed and hopeful young woman I'd been. The one who'd thought that if a lady simply followed the edicts of society and did her utmost to be the genteel ideal, then a future would be easily acquired. No one told optimistic young girls that a future of that sort wouldn't necessarily be bright. Landing a callous duke old enough to be your grandfather did not a happy marriage make. Cawthorn had been mad for an heir, and marrying a ninny-headed chit was an inconvenience required to produce a son. I'd served one purpose and one purpose alone.

But my sister didn't know any of this because I'd never told her. I'd been too embarrassed. Emery was strong and independent, willful, and her own unique woman. As a girl, she'd known exactly who she was and never apologized for it. I'd committed the ultimate sin in denying myself in favor of London society. Emery's resentment and my shame had kept us apart for too long. But now that she and Augie were married and living in town, we were trying to mend our relationship. And over the last year we'd grown closer. But Mary's unexpected blow had guilt rushing hot and heavy in my chest.

Seeing my reaction, Mary scooted forward, her emerald beaded gown bunching. "Damnit, Patty. I didn't mean that."

I sniffed and looked away. "No, you did. And you're right."

Mary clasped my hands tightly, forcing my attention on her. "It will get better. Emery loves you and holds you in the highest regard. Sometimes I want to cry from watching her admiration, so stark and reverent on her dear face. I never should have said that, wielding it like a weapon against you. I'm so sorry."

I nodded.

With a final squeeze to my gloved hands, Mary sat back. "I just want you to be happy, Patty. And I was serious when I said that Miles Griffin could make you so."

"Happiness is not a prize to be won, Mary. You can't rely on someone or something to make it so." *I should know.* I'd thought being the perfect diamond and landing the perfect lord would make me perfectly happy. Relying on anyone was taking a dangerous path. "Depending on Miles to give me happiness isn't fair to me, and it's not fair to him either."

Mary's eyes blazed, the argument ready to explode from her lips. Surprising us both, she took a deep breath before saying evenly, "This is your chance to get what you want, Patty."

I frowned in confusion. "What I want?"

"A baby," she hissed, eyes luminous with emotion.

Shock at her words and her manner caused me to freeze. I couldn't breathe or move. My mouth parted but no words emerged.

"You could have a baby. Even if you didn't want Basilton. You're a duchess and you have more money than God. You could have your family and your friends and a child. A future—one you choose for yourself." Mary's voice was hoarse and imploring.

"How—" My voice broke. "How did you know?" I finally managed. After the husband-hunting and the orphanage visit that had instigated my philanthropy efforts, I knew how desperately Mary wanted a child of her own. I'd never wanted to overshadow that dream. Never intended to diminish her desire by telling her I shared it as well.

Mary dragged a hand down her face. "I went back. I was ashamed of my reaction to seeing those poor children at the orphanage so long ago. So after a while I went back to make a donation. To try to help in some small way. And it had been completely changed. Watford Home for Children, it was called. And it had your hand all over it. I knew you'd renovated it and poured your time and money and love into it. One of the teachers there told me how you visit and spend time with the children regularly. How you care for them. It was obvious, she said. You've changed lives, Patty. I was so proud of you."

A tear spilled from the corner of my eye and I rushed to brush it away.

"But I waited for you to tell me about it, and you never did."

"I didn't want to hurt you," I said, looking down at my hands clasped tightly in my lap. "It was *your* dream."

Mary looked pained by my admission. "Dreams are not owned. I'm not the only woman to have longed for a child, Patty. That's so— I don't even know what to say to that. It's not a competition. Our desires can be one and the same. I'm only saddened that yours has been withheld as much as my own."

"I'm sorry I didn't tell you," I admitted.

"As you should be," Mary said with a smile. "I'm your best friend. I get to be proud of you, and I get to cry with you."

I nodded as two more tears sneaked past my defenses.

We sat in silence for a moment before Mary said, sounding more like herself, "Are you thinking about Basilton?" I groaned at this topic again. "I'm not saying you should use him," she rushed to add. "But if a child came from your arrangement, then what a joyous blessing that would be."

I didn't appreciate even the suggestion of using Miles Griffin to get myself with child. After spending five years married to a man whose only goal was to utilize my body for procreation, the idea of using Miles for the same gains turned my stomach.

"That doesn't make me a bad person," she argued. "Just realistic."

"I do not think you're a bad person. I think, perhaps, that I'm…scared to take a lover." I'd never confessed this aloud before. "I don't want it to be the way it was—with Cawthorn." Somewhere, the hopeful young girl I'd been had been snuffed out by the realism of producing an heir. There hadn't been dancing and romance. There had been thrice-weekly visits to the duchess's chambers when

Cawthorn could manage it. It could have been worse, of course. But that didn't make it any better.

"Do you truly think Basilton would be like that stodgy old crone?"

No, I didn't, so I answered honestly with a shake of my head. "And before you ask, I do not think he's like the rest of The Gaggle or the other men eager for my…acquaintance, shall we say."

Mary snorted. "I'm not saying you need to trust him. Nor am I encouraging you to use him. Perhaps your aims are aligned. At least give him the option and see if he is amenable to an arrangement."

"I'll think about it," I said as Mary opened her mouth to interject. "I will, I swear it. I will seriously consider this option."

For as much as I wanted to deny it, there was something between Miles Griffin and myself. Attraction, surely. And people had become lovers for much less.

Before my mind could run away with thoughts of hazel eyes and strong shoulders, I pulled my attention back to my friend. Her red curls were a riot around her striking face. She appeared her normal self, and yet… "Are we all right, Mary? I'm sorry for keeping things from you."

"Oh tosh, Patricia. It would take a great deal more to harm our friendship." And after a moment, she said soberly, "I truly do wish for your happiness. I know I'm bossy and opinionated and tend to stick my rather large nose where it does not belong, but I always mean well."

"I know," I agreed. And I did know it. I valued Mary's friendship more than she would ever know. Her outrageous personality, humor, and loyalty had pulled me through one of the lowest periods of my life. I wanted nothing more than her happiness as well.

I had Mary and Emery as close confidants. We had a small circle of genuine friends in London. But sometimes it was difficult to remember I wasn't just a lonely widow in a large residence in Mayfair. I'd worn my circumstances as a shield for so long it was difficult to let others slip through the gaps in my armor. I needed to permit honesty with Mary, even if it was hard. I vowed to do better with Emery, and ensure she knew there were no limitations on my sisterly love.

And perhaps I would consider being brave with Miles Griffin.

Seven

MILES

"The line is there, Basilton."

I whipped around to face the elderly man who'd spoken. Marquess Stanton was crowding behind me to place his calling card on the tray in the extravagant foyer. His other hand was pointing to the corridor to my left. A footman had allowed me entry moments before, but I hadn't noticed the marquess's arrival following my own.

"Not a bad lot today," he mumbled.

I snapped my ivory card case closed and noticed for the first time the sheer volume of paper rectangles on the tray. Each name and title were written in plain lettering with very little flourish, but dear God, there had to be thirty of them piled on the silver tray on the wide entryway table.

I'd been distracted by the grandeur of the home, and that was saying something. I'd been invited to well-appointed residences all my life. From the art on the walls to the imported rugs underfoot, Mayfair homes and well-tended country estates were there to impress. But Cawthorn Hall was immaculate. The marble floors and the gilt…well, everything, was simply grand in the extreme. Vases held elaborate flower arrangements on nearly every visible surface in the grand foyer. I took in the high ceilings, and on the way back down my gaze snagged on the ornately framed artwork covering the patterned wallpaper. This did not feel

In a voice devoid of emotion and little volume to speak of, she said, "Get the fuck out." And turned her back to me once more.

~

Several days later, I found myself spoiling for a fight.

Since my return to London, I'd been eager to resume boxing for sport, general exercise, and well-being. It had been an activity I'd enjoyed during my time abroad, and I was looking forward to making it a part of my life back in London. I'd sought out recommendations and found my way to Langham Boxing Club a handful of times thus far. Today seemed like a perfect time to pay another visit.

After the general frustrations of the past few days, I felt rife with tension and disquiet. I'd received another disappointing letter regarding my housing search. And an invitation to the Duchess of Kendrick's upcoming ball led to my most pressing concern: the matter of Patricia.

Following our exchange on Saturday, I'd left Cawthorn Hall against my will and better judgment. The urge to remain and explain myself was nothing short of overwhelming. I'd been desperate to apologize, but the utter disgust and dejection in her tone made me realize several things. Speaking my objections would do nothing but benefit me. Provide *me* solace. Attempt to absolve *me*. Patricia Henney was undoubtedly exhausted by self-serving men. And worse yet, she didn't need another one trying to decide what was best for her. My instinctual reaction would have been defensive at best.

Therefore, I'd kept my mouth shut and done as she'd asked, leaving in a sort of daze while thoughts screamed inside my mind.

Those thoughts were still lobbying for attention. Perhaps boxing would provide a way to focus my unrest. Daly had agreed to attend Langham's and seemed quite enthusiastic at the idea of pummeling me. I tried not to take it personally. Fighting for sport unleashed some primitive male posturing that existed on a baser level. My inner caveman waited in anticipatory glee to exorcise my frustrations upon my competitor. I was sure Daly simply felt the same.

"You ready, then?" Daly asked from within the small sparring ring. He flexed his fingers, stretching the wrappings.

"It's all right. I deserved it for being such an idiot." I didn't specify when or how I'd earned the title, not particularly wishing to discuss my time in Patricia's drawing room.

"Say, perhaps the Duchess of Cawthorn will see your injury and take pity on you at Kendrick's ball tomorrow," Daly added helpfully. I cut him a flat look. "No, you're right. She won't be swayed by a mere flesh wound. But if anything, it will make you memorable."

Ah, if only the duchess could forget some of our interactions. Perhaps we could start over.

Yet the thought of that didn't sit right either. For as surprising and unfortunate as some of our interactions had been, there was still that feeling lingering…that we were somehow more. A vibration along my skin, a knowing in her presence. The spark in her blue gaze when we spoke. I didn't want to forget. And I wouldn't trade all the good just to erase the bad.

As Daly and I removed the linen from our hands and dressed to leave the club, I thought about the persistence of my thoughts today. How attempting to divert myself hadn't driven Patricia from my mind. And how very telling that was.

Perhaps the new Miles—the one I was here and now—didn't need to run and hide from his feelings. Attempting to forget wouldn't change anything that had happened in that drawing room. But perhaps choosing to take action would settle the disquiet. When before, I would have remained silent.

Eight

PATTY

I, Patricia Henney, was nervous.

I could not pinpoint the last time I'd been overcome with anxiety, yet here I was, frantic with an abundance of energy, hands damp with sweat, and eyes constantly scanning the ballroom.

The Gaggle loitered nearby and would likely make a move shortly, but that was not the reason I was on edge tonight at Augie and Emery's event. As much as I was loath to admit it, I'd been out of line with Miles Griffin last week in my parlor. My stomach twisted as I thought about the shock and confusion on his face. I'd permitted my emotions to overwhelm me. I never should have allowed my reaction to become so heated and…visible. I prided myself on a consistently cool outward appearance. The Duchess of Cawthorn did not allow her feathers to become ruffled. My emotions were not available for public consumption. They were private and only permitted in small increments.

Hence the troublesome bout of nerves I was currently experiencing.

After a moment, I took a deep breath to center myself.

Perhaps admitting the cause of my distress—if only to myself—would help alleviate my body's fretfulness.

I was nervous to see Lord Basilton. There. That was the truth I didn't wish to admit.

I was fairly sure he'd be in attendance tonight, and I honestly did not know how to receive him.

Following my dramatic drawing room outburst, I'd assumed we'd have no further contact. He'd left as I'd bid him, honoring my wishes and deflating the anger that had bloomed and prickled like a rose in the garden. I'd expected that to be the very end of Miles Griffin. The odd awareness he brought and that elusive *something* that seemed to connect us was surely severed.

But then, three days later, I'd received a note. There had been no wax seal, no family crest. Just a folded bit of paper.

You're right. And I am sorry.

I didn't need a signature to know it was from the Earl of Basilton. The slanted script and the short message had surprised me. He was consistently doing that. Irritating and unpredictable was Miles Griffin.

I'd kept his short missive on my bedside table, considering the implications of the apology and his acknowledgement. The feeling of guilt from my outburst mixed with the warmth of Basilton's correspondence. The simplicity of his words signaled no expectations, nothing beyond his regret and my truth. But that didn't stop me from considering the repercussions. Was our acquaintance truly over as a result of what had happened? Did his apology mean something more?

And knowing I would likely see him tonight, I'd fretted endlessly.

I'd been busy in the near week since my overwhelming encounter with Miles. Another visit to Watford House had filled a portion of my time. But Emery's ball was the only event I hadn't declined. I loved my sister and wanted to support her. These types of gatherings always made her feel judged and out of sorts—especially when hosting in her own home. Emery wasn't the typical duchess and often felt pressured by her peers and the constant gossip. I'd needed to be here tonight.

And I supposed I would be unable to avoid Basilton forever.

Shifting uncomfortably in my jeweled heels, I scanned the room once more. He wasn't here yet. Emery and Augustus were still greeting guests, and Mary was talking to the Countess Drakefield near the refreshment table.

I didn't have a great deal of time to collect myself before Mary would return with beverages for us both. She would know I wasn't myself.

When I'd been newly in London a decade ago, I'd done my very best to transform into a delicate swan. Every ball or soiree had felt like a performance. Striving for gracefulness and gentility, I'd had goals for my first season. Most young ladies out in society had similar aims. I hadn't been alone in my guileless transformation as I'd attempted to land a suitable match. There was very little pretense because it was all pretense. The season was a game and we were all players.

What I'd confessed to Basilton had been the truth. I'd turned myself into someone unrecognizable in my quest to belong here in London. I'd been a nervous mess back then as well. Biting the inside of my cheek until it bled. Cursing myself for any minor misstep on the road to becoming a duchess.

However, with widowhood came enlightenment. I wore my gowns as armor and kept everything locked up tight behind my walls. These people didn't get the truth of me any longer. They got the image they were presented, a carefully cultivated and unaffected mask.

Miles Griffin had seen behind that mask several times now, and that left me feeling vulnerable and exposed. I was unsure what he'd do with this information. And as much as it pained me to admit, I was biting the inside of my cheek in this particular ballroom because I didn't know how much damage I'd done with my outburst last week. Basilton hadn't been deserving of my ire. He'd merely caught the explosion at the end of a very long-burning fuse. I'd been overwhelmed and, frankly, disappointed to see him among his peers that day. Admitting to myself that I hadn't wanted Miles to be like all the others was painful enough. Admitting as much to him was unconscionable.

I discreetly unclenched my jaw and smoothed my tongue along the abused flesh inside my mouth. Mary was saying her farewells to Lady Drakefield and would be making her way toward me in moments.

A sudden warmth emanated at my side. Without turning my head, I cast my eyes about for the source. I was surprised to find the very object of my thoughts inexplicably near.

"Could we speak for a moment? Alone," Miles Griffin said in a low rasp. He was close and his words moved the fine tendrils of hair behind my ear.

I met his gaze warily, unsure of his intent, but nodded. Mary's surprised expression halfway across the ballroom was the last thing I noted before whispering, "Come with me."

Without waiting to see if he'd follow, I moved toward an interior hallway and bypassed the ladies' retiring room. Moving quickly and finding no other guests in the corridor, I ascended Emery's servants' staircase and eased open the door to the informal family room on the second floor. The fire was banked and the room chilly. I lit a few candles by the mantel and listened as Miles closed the door. The sound was quiet but meaningful. I didn't know how or why but that door closing us inside felt like the start of something—of being on the precipice or approaching a high ledge.

I suddenly felt my nerves in an entirely different way.

I wondered if Basilton could feel it too. Miles still held the doorknob in his hand and faced the barrier between us and the rest of the world. Finally, with what appeared to be a bracing breath, he turned to look at me.

The room was large but it felt dark and intimate, illuminated by few candles. Miles—unmoving by the door—was far enough away that his features were mostly shadowed. He opened his mouth to speak but I felt compelled suddenly—by panic and fear and distance.

I took three steps forward and spoke quickly before he had the chance to say whatever it was he'd blindly followed me in order to say. "I want to apologize for my behavior—the other day. I should not have lost control of my emotions in such a way. I unloaded all of my frustrations of the day onto you and that was not well done of me."

The confession burned with the unmistakable heat and humiliation of being wrong.

Miles took a step toward me. Driven by the pressing need to make him understand, I continued my speech hastily before he could object and demand the floor.

"I'm not, however, sorry for the truth now between us. I meant every word I said." Swallowing hard, I finally looked down at my hands, fingers twisted together before me. "It's probably better that you know my mind anyhow."

Warm strength encircled me, loosening my clenched fingers and cradling my gloved hands gently within his own. "Why do you say that as if it were a bad thing?"

I allowed a ragged exhale before he continued.

"As if your truth makes you somehow deficient." I still couldn't look at him. "How could I possibly hope to know you without getting at the very heart of you?"

My eyes snapped to his suddenly, eager and searching, trying to place his expression. *What does he mean?*

His hazel eyes appeared more gray in this dim light. They regarded me patiently. There was no censure or judgment, just calm resolve.

"I'm still sorry that I lost my temper and ordered you from my home."

"And I accept your apology, although it is not required."

"I shocked you with my outburst."

"You did." He smiled smoothly. "And that is quite the feat."

But I wasn't ready to be swayed by his attempt at levity. "I punished you when what I really wanted was to punish them."

His smile wilted and something dangerously close to pity entered his extraordinary eyes. "And you thought me one of them."

The Earl of Basilton held my hands, and I realized suddenly that I wanted that. Part of my nervousness this evening was in the thought of seeing Miles in the ballroom and being denied…whatever had been happening between us. I had been fearful that my cruel outburst would take away this man as a possibility.

Yes, he'd been an ass. He'd provoked me with his mocking and presented himself as arrogant and insufferable last Saturday. But he'd also apologized. Miles hadn't deserved to be the target of my frustration. His simple note delivered to my doorstep could likely say more than I hoped to convey with my own regrets.

Despite the irritation, the bickering, and the poor first impression, there had been moments between us in the past weeks. Lingering looks and an awareness—a buzz beneath my skin. I enjoyed our verbal sparring, for it could hardly be called a flirtation. Our conversations had never been so frivolous nor playful.

But they'd been *something*.

I liked the wakefulness his presence brought, the way my mind and my body seemed to alight.

And I hadn't wanted to lose that or lose him.

"I'm figuring out that you are not, in fact, like the rest of them," I said, speaking to our joined hands rather than Basilton's handsome face. This felt like admitting defeat. Like surrender on the battlefield.

"Good," he replied simply and released his hold.

I had but a moment to mourn the loss of his touch before I felt his finger beneath my chin, tilting it up as I met his gaze. The pity from earlier was gone and in its place was warmth, comforting and all-encompassing. Miles's eyes held the kind of slow-simmering heat that spoke of patient hands and gentle touches. He was a man prepared for me to shy away like a frightened horse.

And while my heart was thundering in my chest, I'd never been one to back down from a challenge. I returned his stare and raised my chin an inch above, all on my own.

At my stubborn display, his lips turned up at the corners, and that dimple threatened to make an appearance. Miles leaned forward as his gloved hand cupped my cheek. Before I had time to panic over his intent, his lips pressed gently to my own.

He remained still for a moment before layering soft kisses all along the surface of my mouth, from the middle seam to the very corner and back to the top edge. Finally, he nibbled my bottom lip before tugging on it with his teeth. I followed the slight movement and shifted closer, my lips coming flush against his once more while my hands rose to steady myself against his chest.

Miles felt solid, his heartbeat a strong, steady rhythm beneath my palms.

I felt another insistent tug on my bottom lip and I breathed in a gasp, mouth opening at the sensation. Miles took the opportunity to press forward and lick along the part in my lips. His actions seemed both exploration and challenge, in equal measure. So, as with nearly all of our exchanges thus far, I needed to do my part and meet his demands with some of my own.

I darted my tongue out.

He was still cupping my cheek with one hand but I felt the other along my waist, the heat searing and grip firm. I made a small, surprised sound as he deepened the kiss. The feel of his body was so foreign against my own. I craved his warmth as I sought to reconcile our closeness. We fit so well together, his thighs pressed into my velvet skirts. But a growing hardness along my belly had me pulling back, lips disconnecting.

Miles and I were breathing hard, air heated and filling the space I'd put between us. My hands fell away from his lapels I'd been absently clutching as he said tightly, "I apologize. I should not have taken such liberties."

His formality and sudden missishness had me stifling a snort. "I think we've been rather free with one another since the very beginning."

Color high on his cheekbones, even in the waning light, Miles huffed a laugh. "I suppose you are correct."

"What was that?" I asked in feigned confusion. "Can you repeat that last part? A little louder, if you please."

He raised an unaffected eyebrow in my direction but his dimple was on full display. "I don't think so. I wouldn't want you to become unmanageable." A pause, then, "Well, *more* unmanageable."

It was my turn to raise an unimpressed brow.

Miles laughed before canting his head toward the closed door. "Come. Let's return before we are missed."

His movement exposed a shadow on his jaw, purple-tinged and centered between his chin and his earlobe. I stepped forward without thinking.

Startled, Miles turned back to me in confusion.

Pressing up on my toes, I leaned close to better inspect his injury in the dim light. My thumb grazed the area just above the bruising, feeling the evening's growth on his cheek. The intimacy of my unconscious movement had me swallowing nervously before pulling back and lowering to the floor. "What happened?"

Miles blew out an amused breath, his hand rising to rub the back of his neck in a nervous and oddly endearing gesture. "Just a flesh wound." I frowned in confusion. "From boxing," he clarified.

"Ah, I see," I replied, sympathy evaporating. So, he'd asked for his wound.

At my reaction, he laughed once more—the sound more honest and less embarrassed this time. "I knew you would not be impressed."

That, however, had me smiling. I liked that he could predict my reactions, and the fact that he thought about them at all had a warm feeling spreading within.

"To be fair, I was concerned," I argued. "Until I discovered you'd acquired your injury through male posturing disguised as sport. That bruise is a result of your pride. And I find I am not overly impressed by such displays."

Miles appeared thoughtful. "I box for exercise generally. And it was Daly who delivered the blow, if that makes any difference."

I winced. Daly was a powerfully built man. "It does. Now I feel sorry for you."

He chuckled at my teasing and I joined in.

As he carefully prodded his abused flesh, Miles grimaced slightly when his fingertips met the dull purple mark. "Well, if I can't impress you with my manly prowess, I suppose I will reluctantly accept your pity."

"Good," I agreed. Rising once more onto my toes, I pressed a gentle kiss to the bruise on his jaw before backing slowly toward the mantel. We really should return to the ballroom.

Miles eyed me warmly before confirming, "Perhaps less reluctantly."

I smiled as I moved to blow out the candles I'd lit before remembering suddenly. "Wait, you never said what you intended to speak to me about. The whole reason for us coming in here." In my nervousness, I'd monopolized and directed the conversation from the moment we'd arrived.

Reaching for my hand, he placed it on his arm before leading me toward the door. With a smile and quick glance at my lips, he said, "That's all right. I think I expressed everything I intended to."

We descended the stairs and made for the ballroom in silence. Mary and Emery would likely be waiting, but I didn't want to think of them just now. I didn't wish to consider what I might tell them about the time I'd spent alone with Miles this evening. I simply wanted to take in this moment and feel the tension vibrating within, the knowing that unsettled something deep inside me.

Slowing my steps, I cast a sly glance at the Earl of Basilton. My body and my mind felt so very alive. We were poised on the edge of something once more. Our time in the room upstairs had been brash and a touch reckless. But truthfully I didn't mind that he'd crossed the tense divide we'd been hovering on for weeks. Miles might have thought he'd taken undo liberties, but he hadn't. Not really.

I smiled to myself as we turned the final corner back into the ballroom.

He had, however, given me my very first kiss.

∽

Hours later, after the guests had taken their leave and the musicians had packed away their instruments, I sat in the duchess's quarters with Emery and Mary. The traditional rooms for the lady of the house had been transformed following Emery's initial move to London last season. The bedchamber had been redundant as Emery slept in her husband's bed. Therefore, the private space had been reappointed as a studio for my sister. She was a brilliant artist, I'd been surprised to discover. But after witnessing Emery's dedication to her craft, I could understand. Drive and determination had always been her strengths. If my sister wanted to be a painter, I had no doubt she could accomplish whatever level of success she sought.

My friend smiled. "Of course not. But we're not talking about me. We want to know why you are suddenly considering an assignation when you have never been interested before."

I didn't know why this was so difficult to admit—wanting something for myself. I tugged absently on the dance card still tied around my wrist.

"We kissed," I admitted, then took a deep breath. "We kissed and I liked it and I want more of kissing Miles Griffin. There. Are you happy?"

Mary's grin was wide, brown eyes alight. Emery's gaze was more circumspect.

"I, for one, am thrilled by this development," Mary said. "It was my idea after all." I rolled my eyes. "And I think this will be very good for you. Take some enjoyment for yourself."

Emery was being quiet and watchful. I didn't want my typically exuberant and outspoken sister to be so cautious with me. She needed to know she could speak her mind—whatever that might be—and I would still love her. I wouldn't withdraw myself from her as punishment for expressing her thoughts.

Turning deliberately on the settee, I faced my sister. "What do you think, Emery? I value your honesty and your opinion."

Swallowing visibly before she spoke, Emery said, "I suppose I just want you to be happy. And if Basilton will make you happy, then you should pursue this arrangement with him."

"But," I prompted.

Eyebrows drawing low, my sister finally said, "Why do you wish to have an affair with the earl? Do you not wish to marry again someday, Patty?"

I could feel my shock reflected in my features at Emery's unexpected question. I opened my mouth to respond, but nothing came out.

Mary sighed audibly from her armchair and then took a healthy swallow of the remaining sherry.

After clearing my throat, I managed, "I don't know, Emery. I don't know if I shall ever marry again. Honestly, I'm not eager for the prospect, nor for a repeat performance of the past. Conducting an arrangement with Basilton seemed the safest option, and the most agreeable for all involved." A thought came unbidden. "Are you disappointed in me? Do you…think poorly of me for choosing to conduct myself in such a way?"

Reaching for my arm, Emery hurriedly replied, "No. No, of course not, Patty. I could never think poorly of you for choosing your happiness and prioritizing your own wants and desires. I suppose I just want you to find long-term contentment. I'm not saying it has to be with Miles Griffin. But I wish so often for a joyful future for you."

Ah, I could see where this notion stemmed from. "Em, not everyone can have what you and Augie have. Love matches are rare."

"I know that," Emery replied, squeezing my arm gently. "But you have the means to support yourself. Another marriage would be by your own design. You could wait until it was right and true. And I don't know, I thought you and Basilton perhaps had something special growing between you. Beneath all the glares and bodily harm."

I laughed, unwilling to focus on the first part of her speech. I didn't want to think about my first marriage. I'd wished so desperately for a different outcome in that, I couldn't really bring myself to consider what a future union might look like.

"Who knows, Emery? Perhaps something will come out of an arrangement with the earl." Mary's double meaning was lost on my sister.

But not on me.

My sister wished to see me happily wed. Mary supported this affair for a different reason entirely. She was still hopeful that a relationship with Basilton might yield a child for me—something she knew I desperately wanted.

I said nothing as Emery smiled hopefully at Mary's pronouncement.

While a child would be a welcome outcome, that was not the driving force behind my decision. Emery was right. I was prioritizing my own happiness, acknowledging my wants and desires. I remembered warm kisses in a dimly lit room and the press of thighs against my own.

Once upon a time, I'd tried living for a title. For my family. For my peers. For London. For a husband who barely tolerated me.

It was time I lived a life for myself.

Nine

MILES

Lord Basilton,
If you are amenable to discussing an arrangement, I request the honor of your presence tomorrow evening at eleven o'clock. My butler will be happy to escort you from the garden entrance at the appointed time. I look forward to our discussion.
-P

I folded the letter in half before opening it once more to ensure the words hadn't disappeared. I hadn't particularly foreseen the duchess pursuing this course of action, and I needed the reminder of her elegant script to convince me that my eyes had not been deceived.

Patricia Henney wished to conduct a liaison with me. The Duchess of Cawthorn wanted to be my mistress.

Although, knowing her, this was an elaborate ruse to draw me to her lair in order to propose some innocuous partnership rather than the truly indecent pairing I'd been imagining.

Patricia was so restrained and controlled. It was difficult to fathom that she'd allow herself…well, anything really. An arrangement spoke of indulgence and pleasure. I had a feeling the Duchess of Cawthorn rarely allowed herself such things.

Even the possibility of witnessing her giving over to her wants and desires was a heady feeling. To have myself included in those seldom-indulged cravings had filthy fantasies consuming my thoughts and a tightness growing in my trousers.

For someone so self-possessed, what would Patricia's desire look like? Would it be all coaxing words and slow simmering beneath her skin? Or would all her pent-up emotions explode at the first sign of freedom?

I wanted to be there for whatever the night might bring.

Needless to say, I was exceedingly curious. Late tomorrow evening I would saddle my horse and discreetly make my way to Cawthorn Hall and the garden entrance as instructed. I planned to listen to Patricia's demands and go along with whatever she wished.

I knew I wanted her—wanted more than an affair. But she wasn't ready for the truth. I would be shocked if she could admit that she wanted a physical relationship with me. It was not my intent to scare her off with the intensity of my feelings.

I was done with mistresses, finished with meaningless liaisons. But for Patricia Henney, I would take what I could get. I longed to be in her orbit. I wanted her to feel what I felt. What I'd known for some time now. Whatever was happening between us was different. This went deeper than a secret between lovers. I just needed her to see it, to realize that this push and pull between us could be a future. The thread was still there—from that ill-fated first dance—connecting us to one another.

Witnessing her emotional display following her afternoon callers made me realize this passionate woman was so much more than who she presented to London—the town that had shaped her and molded her. I wanted desperately to be in her confidence. These small glimpses at the woman beneath the duchess were the intimacies I craved. I wanted her truth. Ached for sincerity.

I was desperate for the vulnerable woman who cursed on balconies.

And I longed for more surprising kisses and that look of wonder on her face. I'd gone further than I'd meant to in that drawing room at Kendrick Manor, but I couldn't regret it. My fingers flexed involuntarily as I recalled the feel of her, so delicate under my palm. Her sweet taste and soft lips battled any guilt I might have felt at behaving improperly.

Battled and won.

I'd been compelled to act, and the only thing that could have stopped me from kissing Patricia was the woman herself. Just remembering her apology made all of my protective instincts rise to the surface. She'd been so nervous yet determined, her words coming fast, willed into being. I'd hated the thought of her shame. I didn't want her apology. I wanted more of her honesty, but freely given. Not these moments of feeling overwhelmed in my presence, being a silent witness to her vulnerability.

I could never feel sorry for Patricia. She was too strong and capable to wear my pity in any form. However, I felt angry that so much of her life in London had been fraught. Wed to an old bastard. Pursued for her wealth. The mask she wore to protect herself made me long for her freedom.

But that wasn't my place. Not yet anyway.

There was a very good chance that I was farther along than she was on this path to…something. But I was willing to accept that. For now. Patricia had been through quite a bit in her adult life. I didn't know the details of her marriage nor the extent of the cruelty she faced in London, but I knew enough. I hoped with time, proximity, and intimacy, Patricia would realize we could be so much more to each other.

I was willing to wait for that realization. The duchess was not a woman to be persuaded or led to an inevitable conclusion. She needed to reach the idea on her own. It was not my intent to ever pressure her or overwhelm her.

But if I was very lucky, perhaps someday Patricia Henney might be my wife.

∾

"Good evening, my lord."

"Good evening," I returned as I stepped into the short entryway off the garden entrance.

The elderly butler seemed unable to meet my eyes and closed the door awkwardly before clearing his throat and muttering, "This way, sir."

I fought a smile. If this man's unease was any indication, it seemed the duchess did not regularly entertain visitors after hours. That fact gave me a satisfied sort of caveman feeling right in the center of my chest.

Following along in the darkened hallway, we eventually arrived at a large set of mahogany doors on the second floor. After a swift knock, the butler stepped back, taking the candle and most of the light with him.

Barely a second had passed before the door opened and Patricia appeared, looking uncertain and very young all of a sudden. Our eyes met and I smiled.

Her gaze jumped to the butler. "Thank you, Mr. Pitch. That will be all. Have a good evening."

Even in the dim light I could see the flush on the old man's weathered cheeks. He mumbled, "Yes, Your Grace," without making direct eye contact and shuffled back toward the staircase.

Very little light shone from the duchess's chambers. Yet we remained in the dark hallway staring after Mr. Pitch's retreating form before Patricia sighed. "I think I've truly scandalized him."

"Unused to managing callers at this time of night?" I asked casually despite being rather anxious for her answer.

She slid me a look but didn't acknowledge my impertinent question. "Come on," she said finally before grabbing my wrist and tugging me into a sitting room.

There was a fire banked for the evening and an arrangement of furniture before it. A lone candle shone on the table on which it rested along with a low chaise and discarded shawl. Due to the paltry illumination, I could hardly make out the pattern on the furniture nor anything else in the room.

Turning back to Patricia, I took her in. She was a shadow standing in the middle of the floor with hands clasped, dressed in what I assumed was a modest nightgown buttoned nearly to her chin, a cotton dressing gown in what might have been blue wrapped securely around her form. Her pale hair was pulled back in a simple knot at the base of her neck.

Finally, I asked, "Why is it so dark?"

"Because it is nighttime," Patricia quipped.

I gave her a flat look. "I thought I was here for a conversation, Your Grace. Or do you simply plan to have your wicked way with me?" She opened her mouth to respond but I continued, unbothered. "Because I can assure you, if that's your plan for the evening, you'll want to call for more candles. I know, personally, I'd like to see the show."

Even in the near darkness of the room, I could see how her cheeks heated at my scandalous teasing. Patricia looked suddenly very unsure, and I felt the first thread of unease.

My attention snagged on the darkened doorway beyond. I could just make out the suggestion of a bedchamber.

I narrowed my eyes. "You didn't answer me before. I realize I have no right to ask, but do you typically ask your butler to escort gentlemen to your quarters late at night?"

Patricia swallowed visibly. "No. No, I do not." Another swallow, but her eyes finally rose to meet mine. "Actually, you are the first…such…gentleman."

The satisfied caveman feeling returned with a vengeance, but I didn't let my surprise nor my approval show. It was becoming increasingly clear that the duchess was nervous. I wanted her to be comfortable in my presence, and I wanted to give her the pleasure she'd been lacking all these years. If an arrangement with me was the first she'd ever sought, it made sense that she'd be tense. I would do whatever I could to put her at ease.

Perhaps the dim lighting made her feel more comfortable. As much as I wanted to see her body and the pleasure written across her features, I could respect her wishes in this.

With slow, measured steps in her direction, I said very quietly, "Then I will do my utmost to make sure you do not regret your decision."

Patricia's eyes widened as I reached for her ungloved hand.

"Do you want this?" Placing a gentle kiss in the center of her palm, I demanded her honesty. "I need you to be very sure. Because *I* want this." Another kiss on the tender softness of her inner wrist. I left my lips against her skin as I smiled and said, "I very much want to be your mistress."

Her laugh gusted out of her as I'd intended. The tension seemed to melt from her features as she looked at me warmly. I nipped the skin beneath my lips playfully before lowering her hand back to her side.

"I do," she admitted, gaze fixed to my lips. "I do want this."

Keeping my tone purposefully light, I began, "I am a bit curious, I have to admit."

Shaking herself slightly, she stepped back and focused on my eyes rather than whatever indecent thoughts had made her attention stray to my mouth. "What are you curious about?"

Allowing the distance to remain between us, I maintained my position and asked, "Why me? If there have been no others. What made you decide that you might want an arrangement…with me?"

She looked wary, and I cursed myself for questioning this at all. I should have simply said thank you and disrobed.

Finally, Patricia answered, "I suppose I decided it was time." As simple as that. "And it's not as if you're after my money or my hand." She laughed lightly, and I fought the urge to grit my teeth.

I needed to be the man she expected before I scared her off with inconvenient things like my feelings. "That is true," I agreed, and how it burned to play along.

"But there need to be rules," she said, all humor evaporating.

I frowned. "What sort of rules?"

"Well, I assume we both want this…relationship to remain discreet."

I didn't answer. Of course, I knew that any gossip surrounding me with a mistress—duchess or not—would only anger my father. Upon my return to London, the marquess had made it quite clear that my reputation would not survive any more scandal. The less attention I drew to myself in that regard, the better it would be for my stay in town.

But Patricia didn't know that.

I beat back my sudden irritation at being someone's dirty little secret and replied, "Fine. What else?"

If she seemed surprised by my easy acceptance, she didn't show it. "So that means no interaction in public. No more sneaking away from ballrooms together, no approaching me in the park, and no more dances."

With a frustrated growl, I clenched my jaw.

"Can you agree to that, Basilton?"

"I'll meet your demands." She rolled her eyes at my generous tone. "But I think you can call me Miles, Your Grace."

Her eyes had lost that wild panic from earlier and for that I was grateful. Of course she'd take comfort in arguing with me. "Fine. Miles. We're in agreement."

We weren't. Not really. But I'd honor her request.

Closing the distance she'd put between us, I took a step toward her. "We are in agreement, Patricia."

"Patty," she corrected. "I'm tired of being Patricia."

Smiling, I leaned close enough to smell the lavender on her skin before whispering, "Patty."

And then I kissed her. There was no sweet preamble, no teasing nips this time. She'd brought me here for a reason, and I'd seduce her accordingly.

Slipping my arms around her waist, I pulled her close, feeling the heat from her body. Her hands rested tentatively on my shoulders, her tongue cautiously stroking my own. I gentled my pace and moved my palm leisurely up her spine before loosening the pins holding her hair in place. Patty sighed as her hair fell free, and I caressed her scalp, easing the tension from its tight hold.

With slow and drugging kisses, I dropped my hands and untied the sash at her waist. Moving to her shoulders, I pushed the cotton wrapper from her slender shoulders.

After a shuddering breath, Patty pulled back. Before I could protest her loss, she began removing my gloves and tugged me to the dark bedchamber.

I was determined to follow her lead despite my desire to kiss her everywhere, do away with all of her clothing, and light every candle in this room.

She led me to a large four-poster bed. Drawing back the counterpane, Patty dropped my hand and climbed under the sheets. I removed my coat and boots and settled at her side. It was too dark to read her expression, but when I moved to gather her nightgown at the hem, Patty jumped and said quietly, "I'd prefer to leave it on."

I said nothing in response, simply released my hold on the fabric, hoping to ease her skittish nervousness with my immediate acquiescence. After a pause, Patty surged forward. She wrapped her arms around me, her lips crashing into mine. Her kisses were hurried and unpracticed, and another thread of doubt joined the first, giving strength and weight to my concerns. I didn't want a lover who needed to convince herself to bed me. I wanted to earn her affection—to draw her desire forth. This felt like an effort rather than a seduction.

Propping myself on one elbow, I drew back and looked toward her shadowed features. "Are you sure you want to do this?"

"Yes, of course," she breathed.

So, I trusted her. I tucked away my worry and hesitation and I slid my arm around her waist. Vowing to go slow and assuage her obvious anxiety, I placed featherlight kisses along her jaw. Patty sighed and wrapped her arms around my back, bringing our chests flush together. Her softness was a direct contrast to the hard planes of my own body. I skated my hands along her side, eager to feel her breast beneath my palm. She twitched slightly and I paused.

After a moment, Patty encouraged, "Keep going."

My wandering hand resumed its path, and with gentle strokes I grazed her straining nipple through the thin fabric of her nightgown. A small moan escaped the duchess's lips, so I continued my ministrations. Moving my lips along the column of her throat, I kneaded the flesh in my grip, plumping and feeling the weight of her slight form.

I shifted restlessly, my manhood straining the placket of my trousers. I made a small involuntary thrust against where our bodies touched. Another jolt from Patty when my erection grazed the side of her thigh.

Before I could question her response, she whispered, "Kiss me," into the cool night air.

I found her mouth eager and waiting as she ignored my gentle seduction. I nearly lost my composure as her tongue invaded my mouth, licking deeply. Her body trembled with the effort to hold herself back.

My lower body moved reflexively, seeking friction and contact.

Patty sucked on my lower lip and delivered a strong pull before following with a soft bite to the tender skin there. Her hands hadn't strayed from my shoulders and I could feel the tension in her hold.

In fact, it was more than restraint. Her body shook.

The slowly gathering strands of doubt coalesced into one strong thread and gave an insistent tug.

Suddenly I didn't believe her quavering was in response to my prowess at all. Despite the exuberance and effort of her kisses, something was very wrong.

Leaning back onto my elbow and removing my hand from her breast, I asked gently, "Patty?" When her voice never came, I took the silence as an uneasy response and said, "What is the matter?"

A beat before she finally said, breath ragged, "Nothing. I'm— I'm—" And then to my utter horror, she choked on a sob and covered her face with her hands.

Confused and stunned, I sat up. She rolled toward me, crying still. I didn't know if my presence was making things worse, but I ached to comfort her—to ease the pain evident in her cries. "I would like to hold you, but I don't want to upset you further."

Her left hand fell away from her face and she draped her arm around me, nestling into my side. I took that as encouragement and settled down beside her, drawing her distraught form to me. Without speaking, I simply offered comfort and support. She would talk when she was ready or she wouldn't, but I would not force her. Something had triggered this response in her. Women didn't cry during intimacies unless something traumatic made them dread the act or the closeness of another person. I felt quite certain that Patty had experienced something unspeakable in her marriage. But I reined in my mounting anger at the prospect, to be the person she needed here and now as she faced the demons of her past.

With my arms wrapped securely around her, Patty clutched me just as tightly. I stroked her back slowly. Up and down, feeling the length of her spine and doing my best to comfort. I couldn't remember ever feeling so needed—so essential to another person. This heady intimacy—so different than what I'd envisioned this evening—caused my throat to tighten.

Eventually her tears quieted and awareness slowly seeped in. Patty tensed within my hold, so I said in a low voice, "Do not retreat, I beg you. And do not apologize for anything that happened here tonight. If I'd wanted to leave, I would have."

She sighed but didn't pull away. Her explanation came next, tentative and barely audible. "My body got confused, I think. Here in the darkness, it was easy to remember. I don't think of my time in the marriage bed often, but I couldn't seem to control my thoughts this evening. Your touch is not the same, but my mind and my body could not reconcile what was happening between us."

I nodded, my chin grazing her temple. "Did he—" I had to clear the roughness from my throat before continuing. "Did he hurt you?" I finally managed in a measured tone, aware of the damage words could inflict.

"No," she answered quickly. Too quickly. "It wasn't like that. He mostly ignored me. And I suppose that is to be expected when you marry someone decades your junior in order to produce an heir. Cawthorn wasn't rough or hurtful or anything as simple as that. If he had been, it would have been easier to hate him. But there was no affection between us. The act was simply that—an act. An effort to get me with child. There was no kissing nor tenderness. And we didn't have conversations, hardly shared meals together. Becoming duchess was…not at all what I expected."

I remained quiet, sensing she had more to say but needed a moment to collect her thoughts. Truthfully, I needed the time to unclench my fists.

"My body simply remembered. I'm sorry I wasted your time. I'm sorry—"

I cut her off. "No. Do not apologize. There is nothing to be sorry for. I do wish you'd told me, explained your fears so I could have worked to put you at ease. But I understand why you didn't. Your experience was highly personal and who am I to demand your private fears?"

"I was nervous, yes. And fighting against the confusion I felt at being accompanied in this bedchamber once more. But I could not imagine admitting to you how inexperienced in lovemaking I truly am. I suppose I was embarrassed. I wanted you. I *want* you," she clarified and tightened her hold. "But I don't know how to reconcile that. I don't know how to even express that. Our kiss in that drawing room was my first one. Ever."

My body jolted at the knowledge. "Patty." I breathed her name, part astonishment and part plea that this wasn't the truth.

"You don't need to kiss your wife to get her with child."

The words sounded long rehearsed, as if that thought had been a constant reminder but this was the first time they'd been spoken aloud. "I'm so sorry. I would have been gentler—"

Her arm across my chest tightened in censure. "You *were* gentle. It was a wonderful first kiss, Miles. I assure you. I was not disappointed in the least. It was that moment I realized I wanted more affection from you, further intimacies."

"I'm so angry at Cawthorn for treating you thus. For turning your marriage into duty and obligation. He should have worshipped you. And instead he forced you—"

"No," she asserted, rising to look down at me. "He never hurt me or forced me. I was his wife."

"That doesn't make it—"

"I was his wife," she interjected before I could slander his name and recount his villainy. "I was his duchess. I knew my place."

I would have argued but she kept speaking.

"He tolerated my company the best he could in public, and gave me leave to do as I pleased in private. I imagine he would have happily allowed an affair if a child had been the outcome. He visited my chambers and I did what was expected of me. I wasn't beaten or coerced. Toward the end, he was hardly able to perform and his visits were rare indeed. Eventually I think he accepted that I was barren and didn't see the need to bother with me anymore."

She was still looking at me, but I wanted her to hear me—to truly absorb my words. "Patty, you were trained as a woman to accept your due. Just because the old bastard was never violent doesn't mean your life was free of trauma. No part of marriage should be an obligation. I'm sorry you were trapped. I'm sorry you felt like the option before you was acceptable. That it was your due. I don't want you to ever feel that way again."

I couldn't look at her shadowy features for one moment longer. I rose from the bed and went to stoke the fire. As the flames stirred, light filtered into the bedchamber. Now able to see somewhat, I spied candles on the chest of drawers and the mantel. I lit them all. Moving toward a slim desk and a mirrored dressing table, I lit candles there as well.

Shrugging out of my waistcoat, I strode back toward the bed. Patty watched me warily as I climbed in and settled beside her.

"I would light a thousand candles," I told her vehemently. "I would fill every surface in this room to banish the darkness from your eyes. There will be no space left in your mind for anyone else to occupy. I'm claiming all of you for myself. I want you to see me and know that *I* am the one touching you, showering you with the care and affection you deserve."

She blinked quickly and a single tear escaped. Her blue eyes—so brilliant and full of emotion—were hidden from me no longer. I leaned forward slowly and kissed her tear away before pulling her to me. Once more in the cradle of my arms, Patty rested her head on my chest while I breathed her in. There was no urgency in my touch. My declaration had no intent beyond reassurance. Patty needed time before she'd feel comfortable being intimate. I was content to hold her and do my own reassuring—that she was safe and present, no longer fighting her instincts to make herself do something she wasn't ready for.

After a long, comfortable silence, Patty asked, "Are you hungry? Perhaps we could sneak down to the kitchens for some refreshment."

I smiled against her hair. "It is your house, Patty. You don't have to sneak anywhere."

"You know what I mean. I do not wish to rouse the servants."

Ah, yes. I was her dirty little secret after all.

I squeezed her one last time before sitting. "Well then, come on. Lead the way and feed me."

She smiled, and my chest constricted at the sight.

Patty donned her wrapper, covering her ridiculously modest nightgown. I left my waistcoat and boots and quietly descended the stairs in my stockinged feet.

Once we were in the kitchens, Patty located some sort of cake or bread and set to serving thick slices with butter while I made tea. We worked in comfortable silence, passing a knife and filling the kettle. The innocent domesticity had me smiling to myself. If the old Miles—from years ago—could see me now, nearly swooning over preparing a meal with a woman, he'd be very surprised indeed.

Rather than smuggling our wares to the dining room, the duchess and I settled at the worktable in the kitchen. It still had a light dusting of flour that likely never scrubbed clean. I'd stoked the fire when we'd entered, and the large space was warm, bright with candlelight, and smelled of something yeasty and comforting.

I noticed Patty was rather liberal in her butter usage as I took a large bite of the cake on my plate. Fighting a cough, I attempted to swallow. And swallow. And swallow again. However, my mouth was as dry as the Sahara and overwhelmed by crumbs.

Once I managed to finally swallow the offending baked good, I looked to Patty and noticed her restrained mirth. Frowning at the abomination on my plate, I choked out, "What is this?"

Succumbing to her glee, Patty covered her mouth with her hand as her laughter rang out.

"No, really. What is this horrible cake? Is it supposed to be cake? I feel like I swallowed a dustpan."

Her amusement continued until she finally bent at the waist and held her hand up in surrender. "Stop," she managed between inhales. "Stop making me laugh."

"Well, stop trying to poison me."

Laughter renewed once more, Patty buried her face in her hands. After a moment, she collected herself. Wiping her eyes, she eventually said, "I believe it was intended to be apple cake and my dessert from earlier in the evening. I was too nervous to eat supper before your arrival." Upon the admission, her eyes lowered briefly to the worn tabletop.

Eager to banish her embarrassment, I diverted. "Apple cake? Truly?"

Blue eyes met my own as she suppressed a smile. "Indeed."

"Why does it taste like that? Does your cook often serve inedible food?"

"Mrs. Bunce was very fond of the old duke. I imagine she thinks herself loyal to his memory. Or at least his preference for bland and tasteless food." Patty laughed lightly following her statement.

But I didn't.

"Your cook serves you awful food to—what? Punish you?" I asked, incredulous.

Patty fidgeted with the knife balanced on the edge of her plate before saying quietly, "She never liked me much."

"It doesn't matter if she likes you or doesn't. You are the duchess and it's her job to feed you. It's literally her only job. If she misses cooking for that bastard so much, you should sack her. Jesus, Patty. You've been putting up with this spiteful, petty behavior from the woman for years?"

Unable to meet my gaze, Patty said, "I can't just dismiss her. The position is valuable and she's worked for the Henneys her entire life. I wouldn't turn her out. I just couldn't." She sighed deeply and smoothed more butter on her uneaten slice of cake.

She was uncomfortable with my exasperation. It wasn't my place to question her staff nor the household, especially the running of it, but I could not tamp down my incredulity. This woman was a contradiction. She hid her soft heart under a frozen layer of ice and commanded fear and respect in equal measure among her peers. But in her own household she was being run roughshod by an elderly cook.

With what I considered a valiant effort, I took a deep breath and made my tone light. "Well, no wonder you were hoarding all the butter for yourself. Pass it over."

Patty's smile was small and grateful.

We ate our apple cake in comfortable silence while I considered this amazing woman before me. I'd been so drawn to her fierce independence, but discovering her tender and vulnerable nature would be my undoing. I wanted more of these moments—this freedom. In truth, I wanted Patty to be mine.

Eventually we put away our dishes and returned the butter to the larder. When I'd positioned the kettle on the stove, I felt hands suddenly on my back. Patty's curious fingers were smoothing the planes of muscle there through the fine lawn of my shirt. I remained frozen as she explored, touching me how she liked.

I braced my hands on the countertop, letting Patty's nails work their way along my hairline and the column of my neck. A moan escaped before I could control my reaction. But Patty didn't pause in her ministrations.

Her fingers sifted through my long hair and gave a playful tug. "You know, I've been dying to get my hands on this hair. Initially to yank it out of your infuriating head." She laughed and so did I.

"You can pull my hair whenever you like," I said, turning to face her.

Patty's gaze was soft as she ran her fingers along my scalp, brushed strands of hair back from my face and behind my ears. Her eyes drifted from her movements, and I found heat reflected back at me in her stare. "Will you kiss me again?"

I could have refused, assumed that after the emotional events in her bedchamber she wasn't ready for my affection. I was tempted to ask if she was sure, but I decided to trust her to know her own mind instead.

So, in answer, I leaned in and pressed my lips to hers. The kiss stayed soft and sweet as I tasted the apple cake on her skin. Winding her arms around my waist, Patty brought our bodies together in a delicious press. Her hands returned to my back as she stroked and kneaded the flesh there.

My desire grew as our kisses became more frantic and hurried. Stepping closer, I positioned my thigh between Patty's legs. She moved instinctually, seeking friction and pressure on her most intimate places as her lips never left my own.

Her hands on my back became clutching and mindless as her need grew.

Reaching down, I grasped her thigh and hitched it over my hip—opening and widening her stance. Breaking away from her hungry kiss, I whispered, "You can tell me to stop. If I do anything you're not ready for, just tell me to stop. And I will."

I felt her nod, delicate skin rubbing against the day's growth of dark stubble along my jaw. So, with my hand still on her thigh, I lifted and walked us back to the worktable. Placing her gently on the surface, I pressed a hard kiss to her mouth and encouraged her to lie back.

Patty's eyes were wide and confused but she complied. I spread her legs and lowered to my knees before her. Easing one hand along her ankle, over her stockings and to the smooth skin of her inner thigh, I heard a ragged gasp leave her lips.

With the candlelight illuminating myself and my intentions, I slowly lifted her nightgown and parted her wrapper, revealing her creamy skin, inch by delicious inch. In this room that held no painful memories of her marriage bed, I pressed forward and placed a kiss to her knee. Moving deliberately and unhurriedly, I let my lips drag and linger as I shifted ever closer to her center, bared to me from her reclined position on the table.

I peeked a glance over the pale fabric gathered across her hips and found Patty watching me, breath coming fast and lips parted. I gifted her a smile before leaning in and touching my mouth to the lips of her sex. I kissed her the way I had that very first time in the drawing room, nibbling along delicate flesh and eager to feel every part of her.

With a startled yelp, Patty let her head fall back and thump against the table. I smothered the urge to laugh and continued my efforts. With the flat of my tongue, I licked a long, slow line until I reached the little bundle of nerves where her pleasure was concentrated. Another yelp sounded, and then suddenly her hands were in my hair, grasping the wayward strands.

I took her direction and assumed Patty was done with my teasing, so I focused on the apex of her womanhood in an effort to draw forth her climax. I wanted her to know that this was intimacy—not anything she'd been subjected to in the past. Lovemaking could be as simple as seeking the pleasure of your partner for no other reason than it brought you joy. Not to appear too magnanimous, however—Patty's soft mewls and jerking hips were definitely contributing to my own pleasure. My cock was straining and eager.

Suddenly Patty's flesh quivered and pulsed under my tongue, distracting me from the pressure in my trousers. I slipped one finger into her tight channel as her muscles tensed and released. Her moan was low and muffled as she'd draped her arm across her face, eyes clenched shut.

As her crisis eased and reality intruded, I removed my finger from her body and placed one last, lingering kiss to her womanhood, tasting her salt and licking my own lips in response. I stood carefully and lowered Patty's nightgown back over her legs as she remained prone on the tabletop.

Leaning over, I lifted her arm and kissed her sweetly on her cheek. She cupped my jaw and gusted out another breath before speaking, "That was— That was— I don't know what that was."

Patty's eyes finally opened, and she regarded me with slack-jawed wonder. I allowed a devious grin to overtake my features before slipping my arm around her waist and lifting her from the wooden surface.

"*That*," I said with emphasis, "was dessert."

I now knew it was imperative that he remain in good standing with the marquess, and I was sympathetic to his plight. I also desperately wanted him to remain in my bed until morning. These last weeks had been blissful. While we were little more than strangers at society events, several evenings per week Miles would join me late at night and we'd explore our pleasure with one another.

I was still unable to perform the act in this bed. We'd yet to fully consummate our relationship. My body still shook and my mind drifted to the past whenever we'd attempted intimacies in this room. But Miles was patient and kind and inventive. Ever since that first night in the kitchens, we'd made use of the other rooms in the house, freeing my mind from my memories of the duke. Just this evening we'd been in the library. And two nights ago I'd shouted his name while bent over the dining room table as he feasted on my womanhood from behind.

Miles used his fingers and mouth to bring me to climax with regularity and frequency in the last month, and he'd shown me how he liked to be touched as well. I was eager for my body to cooperate so we could take that final step together and experience the intimacy I so often craved.

With reluctance, I released my hold and moved to pull the sheet over my body.

It was his turn to groan. "Don't do that."

My smile was sleepy and satisfied. "What does it matter if I cover myself? You must go."

He suddenly dropped his coat to the foot of the bed and dove under the covers with me. I squealed as he hauled me close, face nuzzling my neck and stealing kisses along my throat to my breasts. "I don't want to leave," he rasped.

I sighed. "I know. But you must. What time is it anyhow?"

"Nearly three," he responded before taking my nipple between his lips.

I gasped for more reasons than one. "Miles! You must go!" This was dangerous ground. He needed to return to his family's home before his absence was noted by nosy servants.

"I know," he murmured against my chest. "I know."

"Have you heard anything from your solicitor about the property near St. James's?

"Yes," he replied sullenly. "I lost the townhome to Lord Eldridge, apparently."

"Oh." It was so odd that Miles had been unable to secure lodgings for himself, especially after months of effort. "Have you spoken to your father about it? Perhaps he's thwarting your efforts and has given his solicitor private instructions."

"I don't know why he'd care. We hardly see each other at the residence, but I can only assume he'd be happy to be rid of me."

"Perhaps your mother wants you to remain in the family home and he's eager to grant her request," I offered.

Finally sitting up, Miles ran a hand through his disheveled hair, looking troubled. "Perhaps," he agreed. "You're right. I should speak with him. I need my own space. I don't want to be under the watchful eye of his loyal staff. And I want somewhere I can be alone. With you." With a hard peck to my lips, he straightened. "I'll see you Friday? Drakefield's ball?"

"Yes," I confirmed. And then remembered what I'd wanted to discuss tonight before I'd been distracted in the library by Miles and his talented fingers. "Oh, there's also the Bartholomew house party in the coming weeks." His brows rose. "Yes, well, my mother is hosting a holiday in Hampshire, at Laurel Park—where I grew up—and you'll be on the guest list. I just wanted to warn you before the invitation arrives this week."

"Patty, are you taking me home to meet your parents?" he said smugly, pausing in his efforts to blow out the candles covering most of the surfaces in the room.

I laughed but it was a shallow thing. Pulling the blanket higher across my chest and neck to hide the creeping flush of embarrassment, I said, "It's traditional. I merely submitted your name for consideration. The marchioness is very exacting. You may not even be invited after all." That wasn't true. I'd asked my mother to include Miles on the guest list before she'd left for the country last week. She'd been confused but happy with my request. Emery had encouraged her by saying what a close family friend Miles had become to both Silas and Augustus as well as herself.

My paramour smiled as if knowing I was bluffing. He moved to stand next to where I lay. Only one candle remained lit—the one on my bedside table, easily within reach. "Well, I shall look forward to the invitation should I be fortunate enough to receive it." I nodded as he retrieved his coat. Leaning forward, he placed a sweet kiss to my forehead and said, "Good night, Duchess."

"Good night," I said, nose stinging inexplicably as I watched him exit my bedchamber. After a moment, I heard the quiet snick of the door to the corridor, and then he was gone.

∽

Nearly three weeks had passed since I'd practically invited Miles to join me for a visit to the country. Mary and I were on our way to Laurel Park to enjoy an early holiday celebration. Augie and Emery were traveling ahead of us. The Earl and Countess Thisby, Mary's mother and father, were in the carriage behind. Marquess Daly was sharing a conveyance with both Miles and my brother, Silas. Mama had invited her close friend Lady Hawkesberry as well. She and her husband, the viscount, would round out the remainder of our house party following their late arrival in three days' time.

Our group would enjoy two weeks of festivities before all nonfamily members would return to London. I was staying on with Emery, Augie, and Silas to celebrate the Christmas holiday with Mama and Father and my youngest sister, Genevieve.

"How are you doing over there?" Mary peered up from the novel she was reading. She held her place with one finger while she regarded me over the rim of her spectacles. She hardly ever wore them—only while reading.

I knew what she was asking and couldn't decide if I should feign ignorance or not. I finally settled on, "Relatively well."

"Relative to what? A carriage accident? Being cornered by The Gaggle? The scent of an alley in the West End?"

"Not quite so dire as all that," I replied.

Placing her ribbon along the valley of the spine, Mary closed her book and set it aside. "Is this truly the first time you've returned home?"

Memories threatened: leaving Hampshire for my first season in London, the excitement I wore like a cloak—masking the young woman I truly was with the person I'd have to become.

"I attended Emery's wedding last year, but I didn't remain overnight. My carriage left obscenely early to arrive for the ceremony and then I slept on the return to London late that night. I wasn't ready for an extended stay at my family's estate. Not then."

"And you are now?" Mary's question was gentle and reassuring.

"Perhaps," I replied. That was really the best I could do. If I'd learned anything from my initial failed attempt to seduce Miles, it was that you couldn't force something that you weren't quite ready to face. Laurel Park had been my home for the first seventeen years of my life. We'd rarely traveled to London in my youth. My father generally preferred life in the country—something Emery seemed to inherit.

But I'd been naively excited for my first season, and determined. I'd made it my priority to be a diamond of the first water and make an excellent match. And I'd accomplished my lofty goals. But I hadn't known at the time what they would cost me.

Returning to Hampshire was difficult for me for a number of reasons. I felt guilt for leaving and staying away for so very long. I had a baby sister who hardly knew me. Seeing Genevieve and how comfortable she was with Emery was painful. Remembering how happy—and how different—I was in the country made me feel shame. I'd changed so much of myself in order to achieve my goals. The reminders would be everywhere.

"Good enough," Mary declared, turning my attention back to her and away from the past. "And how are things with the earl?"

I cut a speaking glance across the carriage.

"What?" She feigned indignation. "I know your relationship with Basilton is a secret, but it's just the two of us here. I'm curious as to how things are progressing. Although, considering his presence two carriages back, I feel it safe to assume that things are going rather well."

I said nothing.

"And should you feel the need to express your gratitude for my truly genius idea, I'm happy to accept those little French chocolates they sell in Fleet Street. You know the ones. With the raspberry filling."

I laughed at her absurdity. "All right. All right. Things are going well between myself and the earl. We are…getting to know one another better."

Mary frowned in confusion. "Getting to know one another? As in…what-he-looks like-without-his-clothes-on better?"

"Mary!" I exclaimed, hiding my laugh behind my hand.

"Because that was the whole reason for this endeavor and my encouragement. I didn't intend for you to gain a new friend. I wanted you to enjoy bedsport with that man. It's only right. It's what you deserve."

I was still grinning. "You're ridiculous. And I *am* enjoying myself. He's…not what I expected."

Mary's eyes narrowed before she gasped. "Oh no, Patty! Are you falling in love with Miles Griffin?"

"No," I replied, laughing at her horrified expression.

I wasn't falling in love with Miles Griffin. I was… I was…enjoying his company. We talked. And he made me laugh. He listened to me and didn't judge me. It was a rare man indeed who could be free with his affections and loose with his demands. Miles never pressured me for anything—not for intimacies and not for explanations. Yet he was still the only person on this planet who knew so much about my marriage. I trusted him with the knowledge. I trusted him with quite a bit actually.

"Oh no," Mary wailed. "Your face. You're having a realization right now. It's like watching a cloud uncover the sun, one summer breeze at a time."

I sobered immediately. "You're wrong. I was simply thinking. I'm not in love with the man. Don't be absurd. We spend half our time together arguing."

"But you like that," she accused.

I pursed my lips rather than contradict her. I *did* like that. Now we argued with less clothes on. And I liked that too.

But I didn't love Miles.

Did I?

I attempted to isolate my emotions, and considered what a heart *should* feel like when occupied by another. I didn't actually know.

I swallowed and looked at my friend. She was still staring at me, wide-eyed behind her spectacles.

"I don't love him. He's my mistress," I joked.

She didn't laugh, just continued regarding me worriedly. Before she had time to voice any more concerns, the carriage jerked to a stop. I glanced out the window. In my distracted state, we'd arrived at Laurel Park without me having noticed our approach.

A nervous tightness entered my stomach and I pressed a hand there to quell the sensation.

"Patty"—Mary leaned forward, poised on the bench across from me,—"are you going to be all right?"

Removing my gaze from the window and the estate beyond, I opened my mouth to assure her that *of course, I will be fine*. However, the carriage door opened just then, and Miles was there, armed with a fully dimpled smile.

"Ladies," he greeted happily. Mary returned his salutation but eyed me warily.

Miles helped us descend from the carriage. For a brief moment, I closed my eyes and breathed in the cold December air. It was fresh and crisp and made me think of snowy, gray winters with my sisters and brother.

"Are you ready?" Miles said quietly, tucking my fur stole snugly under my chin.

"Yes, of course." I slid my hand over the soft, dark wool covering his arm and we joined the others on the front stairs.

My mind was spinning between thoughts of home and memories from the past. And I had the added confusion regarding the man at my side to contend with.

But with a few quiet words, spoken only for me, Miles helped clear the cobwebs and alleviate the pressure I'd felt but moments ago. "I must admit, I'm actually quite nervous."

My gaze snapped to his. Those hazel eyes reflected the gray cloud cover and fairly glowed against his dark coat. "Why?"

Miles released a deep breath. "I don't know. I'm just finding it difficult to be my usual charming self."

I rolled my eyes.

"No, truly," he insisted. "I want to make a good impression."

I smirked. "Don't worry. I didn't tell my mother how insufferable and irritating you were when we first met."

"Oh, thank God."

I laughed, drawing Emery's attention as she turned to give me a happy grin. We were nearly to the front door, waiting as my mother greeted Lord and Lady Thisby.

I could hear Silas teasing Mary over her spectacles that she'd forgotten to remove as they occupied the stairs directly behind us.

Pausing on the step beside him, I faced Miles and noted his odd expression. Perhaps he *was* nervous. I'd never seen him look so unsure.

The thought of returning to Laurel Park didn't make me quite as anxious and fretful in this moment. I could ease the way for Miles, focus my attention on introducing him to my family and my home. The pressure to return to this estate as a missing piece had been weighing on me for weeks. But realizing I no longer fit the space I'd left behind wouldn't be as devastating with this man by my side.

Miles had never known Patty Bartholomew, whereas my family still remembered and mourned the loss. One could never win when competing with a ghost. Perception outweighed truth every time.

With Miles, there was no nostalgia to contend with, no expectation to be someone I no longer was. He wasn't waiting for me to come home. To him, I was enough.

I tugged him up to the landing as my mother ushered in the rest of us out of the cold, and whispered to him sincerely, "Never fear. I'll protect you."

∽

Dinner was a boisterous affair.

Rather than retiring to our rooms upon arrival, we'd gathered in the drawing room for light refreshment before I'd taken Miles on a tour of the house. We'd meandered for a long while with me pointing out Emery's artwork and some of my favorite memories and stories associated with my former home.

Now, my brother, Silas, was dominating the conversation, entertaining our mother with his theatrics. Father was listening politely as Emery attempted to interject and correct something Silas had said. Daly was conversing with Augustus, who was looking on the scene in quiet amusement, as was his way. Lord and Lady Thisby seemed charmed by Miles who was seated beside them. Mary and I observed from across the table where we sipped our wine between courses.

"Basilton is quite the dinner companion," Mary murmured for my ears alone.

"I think he was relieved to be seated next to your parents rather than mine," I said before Mary cut me a quizzical glance. "It seems he's a bit nervous," I explained.

"That's rather adorable," my friend replied with a surprised smile.

We turned our attention back to the conversation taking place before us.

Sometime later, during the fish course, Silas asked curiously, "Where is Genevieve?"

I had assumed she didn't want to eat dinner with the stuffy adults and preferred to dine with Julian in the informal dining room. My little sister was quite close with the housekeeper's son. They were near in age, both having just turned sixteen in November. Julian had practically been raised here and had been educated alongside Genevieve. They had always been two peas in a mischievous little pod.

Some disquiet was moving down the dining table at Silas's abrupt question. My mother appeared uncomfortable and Emery looked morose.

"What is it?" I said, sudden concern bleeding through my tone.

Mama seemed surprised that I was the one inquiring, and her blue eyes—so much like my own—widened. "It seems Mrs. Moore secured an apprenticeship for young Julian with her brother at a farm in Leicester. He departed a fortnight ago. Genevieve is..." My mother paused before casting a cautious glance at the Thisbys. "Still adjusting, I'm afraid."

Oh, no. Poor Gen. I could not begin to imagine how difficult this separation would be for her. She and Julian had been devoted friends their whole lives, and Emery had confided in me our sister's wish to someday marry the housekeeper's son. Their relationship had been quite innocent, and Genevieve's feelings had been a secret to everyone save Emery. She must be devastated.

Gen and I were not close, not really. And that was my fault for being an absent older sister. But I loved her and wanted her to be happy. Perhaps she'd like to come stay with me in London to help take her mind off Julian. She'd be out in society in the next year or two, and she'd seemed to enjoy herself upon her last visit to Cawthorn Hall when she'd accompanied Mama and Emery last spring. I would speak to Emery and see if she thought it was a good idea.

I glanced to my sister as my thoughts spun with ways to improve this situation. Conversation had yet to resume since my mother's subdued tone relayed the news of Julian's departure. Emery met my eyes and guilt flashed briefly across her face.

I frowned, unsure, but then Emery spoke. "I received a letter from her last week explaining the situation. I'd hoped our presence here would cheer her somewhat. I'll seek her out this evening."

Ah. So she felt guilty that Genevieve had confided in her. I did not begrudge Emery her closeness with Gen. I was happy they had each other for support after my move to London all those years ago. But it stung a bit now that I was trying to make amends for the distance I'd put between myself and my sisters. I needed to remember that our relationship would not be rebuilt overnight. I would keep trying. Emery needn't feel shame because Genevieve trusted her enough to confide in her.

I nodded and gave a small, sad smile at the news.

Silas agreed, "And I as well. I think you're right, Em. With all of us in residence, we'll be able to distract her. Speaking of distractions…" And then he was off with another story to brighten the mood his innocent question had unintentionally diminished.

I looked away as my thoughts turned toward guilt and the complexities of coming home again. Miles caught my gaze and frowned in concern at whatever expression I was wearing. Shaking off my melancholy, I attempted a bright smile that only made his brows drop lower. Just then the servants approached with the roasted leg of lamb, and in the moment of distraction I looked away from Miles lest I trouble him even more.

For the remainder of our meal, I was able to eat quietly and contribute very little to the overall conversation. But as I was taking my first bite of Mrs. Pennyworth's festive and delicious plum pudding, my mother's voice carried across the table.

"Patricia, darling, I can't wait to show you all the improvements we've made to the property since you were last here."

I winced at the insinuation. I'd been gone too long and needed a tour of my own family home.

"And I'm sure you're unaware of the changes and growth in the nearby village. The shops make for an enjoyable day trip."

"Yes, Mama. That sounds wonderful." I'd aimed for cheerful in my response and landed somewhere in the vicinity of false brightness.

My mother didn't seem to notice, however. "If we can manage to get you to return in the spring"—she laughed indulgently—"you'll be amazed by the gardens here at Laurel Park. They are a riot of color and some of the most beautiful around."

My heart was beating so forcefully, I could feel it in my throat. Realistically, I knew I would not be able to ignore my absence here for the last near-decade. It was unreasonable to assume my mother could accomplish this feat. I knew she was not malicious in her reminders. Yet my defensiveness was ingrained. I felt like a failure—an unfeeling daughter, an absent sister, an utter disappointment.

Nodding, I finally said, "I'm sure you are very proud."

Swallowing awkwardly, I realized I still held my spoon poised over the pudding dish. A quick glance around the table showed my smiling mother as well as the painfully sympathetic faces of Emery, Augustus, Miles, and Father.

All at once, Mary, Emery, and Miles started speaking, each changing the direction of the conversation and pulling the attention away from me. Their sweetly protective instincts had me fighting a smile while at the same time feeling weak for requiring saving.

I pushed the pudding around my plate until the meal ended shortly thereafter. The ladies were retiring for sherry and gossip while the gentlemen were accompanying my father to the library for cigars and brandy.

However, I didn't think I would be able to produce passable conversation nor convincing smiles, so I wished everyone a good night and declined after-dinner refreshment due to fatigue and a headache from traveling.

Miles watched me with a worried expression before I nodded encouragingly and finally turned for the staircase. Making my way to the family wing, I admonished myself for my behavior. There were likely going to be several occurrences over the next few weeks that would cause my ever-present guilt to flare. I needed to make peace with the past and live the life I wanted now.

The problem was I didn't know how to stop punishing myself for my mistakes. I would simply try to remember that, much like my relationship with Emery, I couldn't expect change to happen overnight. I needed to be patient with myself and my expectations for this holiday. Every comment from my mother was not meant as an attack. I shouldn't take them as such.

With a deep breath, I opened the door to my old bedchamber. The hinges still squeaked horribly if you opened it more than halfway. I winced at the sound, and a muffled shout came from within. There was no fire lit within, and the startled figure wedged between the armoire and the dressing table was another clue that something wasn't quite right.

My little sister Genevieve was cast in dramatic shadow by the lone candle in the room. Illumination from the hallway sconces bled into the open doorway as I asked softly, "Gen?"

"Oh, you startled me." She sniffed and discreetly wiped under her right eye.

"Are you well? What are you doing hiding on the floor?"

With a glare aimed my direction, Genevieve said defiantly, "I'm not hiding."

"My mistake," I agreed easily and walked slowly toward her after closing the bedroom door behind me. "Do you know why none of my things are in here?"

She looked at me like I was mad. "Did you truly think Mama would make you stay in your old bedroom? You're a duchess. She put you in the Red Suite."

"Oh." The red room was for company. It was in another wing on the second floor and typically housed the highest-ranking guest during house parties and holidays. I felt strange—both honored by my mother and disappointed that she'd removed me from the family wing. "Is this your room now? I'm terribly sorry for intruding. Mama never said where I would be staying. I simply assumed I'd be here—with all of you."

Genevieve eyed me curiously. She looked very young and very untrusting, but at least her eyes were now dry. Imagining her grieving in here in the dark instead of at the dinner table with her family made my chest constrict in sympathy.

Finally, she admitted, "No, this isn't my room. I was just in here…thinking."

Lowering myself in a cloud of skirts, I sat in front of her. Not so close that she'd be overwhelmed, but not so far that she could ignore me. "I do my best thinking on the floor."

She remained skeptical as she watched me, so I watched her right back. Her dark blond hair was curled and styled away from her face. She'd grown since last year—as children were wont to do. Her face had lost the roundness of youth, and her figure reflected the woman she was becoming.

I was reluctant to bring up Julian, knowing the subject would likely upset her.

"You can ask," Gen said matter-of-factly. "I'm sure Emery already told you."

"She didn't," I replied gently. "Mama mentioned Julian leaving at supper."

"Julian didn't leave," she snapped, sadness evaporating. Or perhaps transformed into something else entirely. "He was sent away. From his home. From everything he knows. And from me."

"I'm sorry, Genevieve. That must be very difficult. For you both."

"I wouldn't know. I've written to him every day. And he hasn't written to me even once, despite promising he would. I don't know anything about how it is for him."

I desperately wanted to take her hand and squeeze, offer support, bring her some cake, something. However, I was very much a trespasser in this private, emotional battle she was waging.

"Perhaps he is still getting settled or the post has been delayed," I finally settled on. She was back to scrubbing under her eyes, and I felt horrible for making her discuss this. "I am certain Julian will write to you soon. Have you asked Mrs. Moore if he's yet arrived in Leicester?"

Gen snorted derisively. "She's not likely to tell me anything. She hates me. I'm the reason he got sent off."

I frowned at my sister's vehement assertion. Mrs. Moore had been with our family for ages. She'd been the housekeeper at Laurel Park for as long as I could remember. Not terribly friendly. A rather hard woman, all told.

"You don't believe me," Genevieve accused.

"That's not true. I just wonder what makes you feel this way. Has Mrs. Moore mistreated you or hurt you?" I asked.

"No. Nothing so bold as that. I've heard her talking to Julian. I know she hates me, and always meant to keep us apart."

I kept my tone even. "That sounds very spiteful indeed. What did Julian have to say about that?"

Genevieve bit her lip as her eyes filled. After a moment, she finally managed, "Jules always made light. Said it didn't matter how she felt. That I would always be his best friend."

Oh, darling girl.

My poor sister's pain was undoubtedly amplified by Julian's disregard. Her feelings were likely much stronger than his. She must be suffering unbearably, not just by the loss of him in her life but by the loss of the future she had dreamed of.

"What should I do, Patty?"

I was startled by the quietly uttered question. I couldn't believe she would ask me for advice about anything. "I think…" I hesitated, gathering my thoughts, suddenly anxious to say the right thing. I considered what had given me a sense of purpose when I was lonely and miserable in London. Watford House and the children therein had been my refuge, my saviors. "I think you should give him time. Keep writing to him. Don't give up on Julian if you do not wish to. No matter what anyone says. And in the meantime, fortify your heart, find a cause you love—just for you—and cling to it. Do you have something like that?"

My sister finally stopped speaking to her lap and gave me a shy glance before saying, "I enjoy writing. Adventure stories and romance. Mysteries. I love to read as well, but something just compels me to create characters and stories of my own."

"I think that's amazing," I said genuinely. "Focus on your writing. Don't stop. Even when the world feels like it is crumbling around you. Keep this for yourself. A secret freedom that cannot be taken from you."

The candlelight flickered and shadows danced across Genevieve's determined features. She looked both young and wizened. Most of my memories were of a very young child—shy and sweet and desperate to be included with her sisters. But Genevieve was a young woman now—her own person.

I'd been so focused since my return to Hampshire on all that I'd missed and all that had changed in my absence. And yet, in this moment, Genevieve needed the advice of the woman I was today—the one who'd left, naïve and trusting, and returned someone wiser and a bit harder. Perhaps my sister could learn from my mistakes.

With a hand braced on the floor, I rose carefully to standing. Brushing out my skirts, I smiled. "I'll leave you to your thoughts. I'm sorry, again, for interrupting. Good night, Genevieve."

"Good night, Patty. I'm…glad you're home."

Her words had tears burning the backs of my eyes, but I smiled instead. The reminder of my time away didn't pinch quite so sharply when uttered by Genevieve in my old bedroom. They felt like a gift, a truth passed between two women who were busy fighting ghosts.

I left my sister to her misery. I'd intruded long enough. When a broken heart needed mending, sometimes you simply had to hold the needle and thread yourself.

Eleven

MILES

"Dammit," I breathed as the hot wax dripped down the side of the candle right onto the tip of my thumb. Switching hands, I paused to scan the empty hallway, hoping no one heard my foul exhalation.

Quietly and carefully I resumed my path down the corridor to the family wing. This was an idiotic idea, to be sure. However, I needed to check on Patty after the stressful events of dinner. Watching her retreat and pull away from all conversation had been difficult to witness. And our separation down the length of the dining table hadn't helped matters. I wanted to reassure her, squeeze her hand discreetly out of view, and direct the discussion away from her past. Anyone could see it made her uncomfortable. Her mother's insistence on bringing up painful subjects would only succeed in driving her daughter away.

I didn't particularly know how I would find Patty's room among those in the family wing. There wasn't likely to be a sign upon the door, but perhaps a clue or instinct would lead me to the correct one at this late hour. I was being entirely inappropriate, but I could also be very charming. If a servant happened upon me, I could likely talk them into Patty's current location.

Suddenly, the creaking of a seldom-used door hinge had me freezing in place. A moment later the Duke of Kendrick entered my field of vision and the pitiful light cast by my single candle.

wanted to erase the barriers between us, and hoped that at some point in the future she'd turn to me for comfort rather than hide herself away.

With a deep breath for courage, I raised my hand to knock quietly. Yet before my knuckles made contact, the door suddenly jerked open and there she was.

In her lavender dressing gown cinched at her waist, Patty stood before me with a smug expression. "Were you going to stand there all night?"

I smiled as she grasped the lapels of my waistcoat and pulled me into her well-lit room. The fire was blazing, and the red guest suite was warm and inviting. Lavishly appointed, the room came very close to being ostentatious. I was sure Patty would have preferred her quarters in the family wing.

Closing the door quietly, I allowed her to lead me, pulling me toward the rather large canopied bed. Red velvet draperies hung along the frame with only one side pulled back to reveal rumpled bedclothes.

"Did I wake you?" I asked as my steps followed her ever closer to the bed.

"No, I was reading, wondering if you'd pay me a visit this evening. And then I heard your footsteps and saw the light from your candle beneath my door." Her smile was coy and made it clear what she thought I'd be visiting for.

I tried to quell the disappointment I felt at her assumption that I was merely here for intimacies—daring and eager in this new environment. "I wanted to check on you following dinner. Are you all right? I know your mother's remarks were—"

Suddenly Patty was kissing me. She took my words and concern and swallowed them down. I allowed this misdirection, for it was not my intent to bring her more pain and discomfort. But I'd be lying if I said the attempt at diversion didn't sting.

Patty asserted her will and deepened the kiss, all the while tugging me closer to the bed. Her eager fingers went to work on the buttons of my waistcoat and she pushed it impatiently off my shoulders.

I threaded my fingers through her pale blond hair. It was soft and delicate and moved over my hands like silk.

Attempting to slow the pace of…whatever this was, I gentled my kiss. Placing teasing nips along her lips, I worked my way slowly down the column of her throat, the skin smooth and sensitive to my touch.

Patty's hands were still straining against my torso, lifting my shirt from my body. Separated momentarily by the movement, I paused. Instead of resuming my path to her collarbone, I pulled her into my embrace. I simply wrapped my arms around her and held on tight.

After a moment, Patty's arms closed around my waist and she returned my hug, clutching me with a sense of desperation. "I'm so glad you're here, Miles." The words were breathed into the bare skin of my chest where they branded themselves across my heart.

"I'm glad I'm here too," I admitted, pressing a gentle kiss to the top of her head.

Our movements became slower after that. Patty's urgency had transformed, the intensity channeled into shaking hands and broken pleas.

When she undressed me further, her lips traced patterns onto my flesh that only she could see. She took her time, her soft hands smoothing the planes of my body. With equal patience, I untied the wrapper at her waist and pushed it gently down her arms where it pooled on the floor. My lips finally found her collarbone as I traced a line of heat with my tongue. Patty's soft moan at the contact had my cock twitching painfully against her nightgown.

Eager for the feel of her bare skin, I reached down to grasp the fabric and pulled it up and over her head. Patty smiled as her long hair settled back over her shoulders, gloriously nude before me. Before I could resume kissing or touching her body, she reached for my hand and bid me to lie back across the white bed linen.

Patty followed me down upon the mattress, but instead of settling at my side, she straddled my hips and lowered herself until our centers aligned. I made an involuntary sound at the contact. Her heat was astounding as my cock nestled against her folds.

We hadn't done this before. In our nearly two months of exploration, Patty had never taken the lead this way. And I'd been determined to wait until she was ready before we consummated our relationship and crossed the final threshold in our lovemaking.

She gave a small experimental thrust, sliding easily against me. The movement had my eyes rolling back in my head as my hands went instinctively to her hips. Unsure of my touch, I loosened my grip, preparing to pull away altogether. But she was there. Reaching and covering my hands, Patty guided them back to her hips as she continued moving over me. "You feel so good," she said on a ragged exhale, and I thought this might already be over for me.

I tightened my hold and pulled her close. The friction was equal parts maddening and exhilarating. She was close to release. I knew the signs. But before her eyes lost focus, before she could breathe my name the way she always did—reverent and infinitely arousing—she paused and looked right at me, a question in her gaze.

"Can we? I—I'm ready."

I froze, fingers flexed on her slim hips. "Are you sure?"

She nodded quickly. "I am."

Swallowing hard, I said, "You are in charge. Stay right where you are. Do whatever feels good." Patty nodded. "And if you need to stop, it's all right. We can try something else." I smiled, so she'd know I was sincere. My cock had never been this hard and my body was ready to explode, but if Patty needed to stop, we would. And that would be that. I could wait on her—on this. It was more important that she be comfortable in bed with me than anything else.

I didn't know what had given her the confidence to take this step. Whether she'd finally grown relaxed with the idea of intercourse, or if the new surroundings had been enough to instigate the change.

But I trusted her. Ached for her. And I'd be whatever she needed.

She rose on her knees and met my gaze. "Will you help?"

Reaching down, I fisted my erection as she slid back. The urge to grasp her hips and thrust up and into her warm body was admittedly strong, but I refused to force my will. This needed to be about Patty.

Slowly—so fucking slowly—she inched down onto my cock. I was enveloped in her snug embrace as she worked to accept my invasion. When she was finally seated and could go no farther, Patty's wide eyes transformed. Her expression became triumphant and we both laughed aloud at the same time.

"Give me your hands," I said finally, aching for her to move, desperate for her touch. Patty complied and I placed her palms on my chest as her hips tilted forward. She gasped at the change in position, and I felt her intimate muscles clench around me. "Now use me. Brace yourself against my body and move however you like."

Her tentative thrusts had me biting the inside of my cheek, but soon she found her rhythm, her pace increasing. I wasn't going to last much longer. She felt too good. Too hot and wet.

I brought the pad of my thumb to where we were joined, and found the place that made her squirm. Her movements faltered for a moment before she recovered. I continued circling her apex with one hand and brought the other around to squeeze the globes of her ass.

She became erratic and wild as she neared her crisis, and when I felt her inner walls squeezing, I reached up, bending in half as I brought my arms around her, holding her close to me. I thrust up into her body as Patty moaned her release, my name escaping on a harsh breath. Pulling her in tight, I pumped once, twice more, before spilling within.

When I came back to myself, I was still sitting upright with Patty on my lap. Her arms were wound around me and her hands played in my damp hair. I kissed her collarbone, the only place within reach.

Looking up with sleepy, pleasure-drunk eyes, I took in Patty's radiant expression. She brought her lips to mine and we kissed deeply. She drank me in, and poured every ounce of her obvious pride into that kiss.

And, in turn, I poured every ounce of my love.

∽

"Now that is delicious," I said after licking my fingers clean. The flavor, somehow both tart and sweet, lingered on my tongue.

"Isn't it?" Patty agreed, lips wrapping eagerly around the segment she was holding.

I peeled apart another section of orange and brought it to her mouth. She smiled before snatching it from my waiting hand. Her teeth scraped purposefully along my thumb and I raised a challenging brow as she laughed.

I didn't know how to describe her mood. It was the most free I'd ever seen her. Patty seemed buoyant and light, laughing and smiling easily as we lounged naked, eating fruit in her bed. I didn't know if our lovemaking had prompted her temperament, or if she—like me—simply enjoyed our easy way with one another.

"My mother was thoughtful to bring these over from the orangery. They've always been my favorite."

I eyed the basket of orange fruit atop Patty's dressing table and couldn't help the intrusive thought that if the marchioness had any awareness about her child at all, she would have welcomed her in the family wing of the house instead of delivering citrus to her in this well-appointed guest suite.

I decided to gently introduce the topic of her family. "That was kind of your mother to remember your favorite fruit."

Patty eyed me, but the smile didn't leave her face. "You can say what you wish to say, Miles."

I attempted to make my expression entirely innocent, and she laughed, as I'd hoped.

"I just wanted to make sure you were all right, you know. That's why I sought you out this evening. Not that I'm complaining, but it was not to seduce you in your bedchamber."

Patty gasped in mock affront. "I believe I seduced you, my lord."

I smiled. "Indeed you did, Duchess."

"I'm…" Her face didn't fall, but it was a near thing.

I suddenly felt like an arse for dimming her light and asking her to discuss difficult subjects. But I needed her to know I cared about her—beyond late-night seduction. This was more.

"I'm better than I expected. Being here is difficult. I haven't stayed overnight since I left for London, before my first season. Laurel Park and my family, at times, make me feel guilty and inadequate and one thousand other complicated emotions. It will get easier, I know this."

Considering something, I asked gently, "Does Silas feel as you do?"

"What do you mean?" Patty asked, frowning in confusion.

"He's unwed and without an heir. I know he rarely returns to London or Hampshire, and prefers to spend his time on the Continent. Does he trouble himself with what your mother and father think? Are they disappointed in his choices, for remaining abroad?"

"No, of course not," she replied. "Mama does scold him occasionally, but it's mostly in jest. She just wants him to be happy."

With my voice as soft as I could make it, I asked, "Then why are you so hard on yourself, Patty?" She didn't answer or argue, so I continued. "Yes, you've stayed away, but you're here now. You're mending your relationships. You're doing your best. Believe that it's good enough for your family…and let it also be good enough for yourself."

She nodded once and looked away. "I see your point." After a moment of silence, still worrying the orange peel on the plate between us, she admitted, "Honestly, I've found it easier to be here…with you."

I met her shy confession with sincerity. "Why do you think that is?"

She blew out a breath. "Probably because you never knew me as Patty Bartholomew. You lack any preconceived notions about how I'm supposed to act or who I'm supposed to be. It's quite freeing to be in your presence, actually."

"I'm glad of that. Truly."

Finally raising her gaze, she said thoughtfully, "Honestly, you've never asked me to be anyone I'm not. You're ridiculously unflappable. I fear you're just what I need."

My heart was pounding with the need to tell her. To just say, *I love you. I love who you are, here and now.* But I knew Patty wasn't ready for that. So I strove for lightness. "You know, I've liked every version of you. Even the one cursing me on a balcony in the dark."

She laughed. "I wasn't cursing you specifically."

"You're right. That would come later."

Patty smiled.

I felt I owed her some honesty in return. I'd been rather eager to share my opinions regarding her family and her return home, but perhaps I wasn't being fair.

"You know, I do have some experience returning home after several years away." Patty and I had never really discussed my absence from England.

Watching me curiously, she said, "That's right. You mentioned it on the night we met. You'd returned from France."

"I did. My father sent me away six years ago."

Patty frowned. "Sent you away?"

"Yes." I fidgeted with the orange segment I still held, the sticky juice painting my fingers. "You'd probably just lost your husband, so you likely do not recall the gossip surrounding my exile. But I'd pushed my father too far for his morals and principles. Drawing attention for carousing threatened his reputation and he went farther than I ever anticipated."

Reaching over, Patty stilled my nervous movements and replaced the fruit with her own hand, lacing our fingers together. "What happened?"

I sighed. "An article was printed in the *London Post* about my hedonistic ways—being seen openly in society with my opera singer mistress, flouting my misdeeds, and dragging my religious father's name through the London filth. Our relationship had always been strained. I could never quite manage to be the heir he wanted. Even as a child. I had a stammer that used to infuriate him. I grew but my affection never did. We remained at odds throughout my entire adolescence. I was young and antagonistic, resentful of the marquess and his demands on our family. I was immature. I can appreciate that now."

"So he sent you—his heir and only child—away for six years?" Patty was incredulous.

I smiled with little humor to speak of. "It was a sound punishment."

"What about the Basilton estate and funds? You are wealthy beyond the Salisbury allowance, of course."

I tried not to feel the familiar bitterness that came from Patty's reminder of my means. I knew she used that as an excuse to continue our arrangement. I didn't need her money, therefore I could be trusted. Unlike the rest of the men who sought her out.

I cleared my throat before saying, "He banished me from the life I enjoyed. He knew I'd never seek the country estate in Gloucester entailed to my courtesy title. I'd always preferred life in town. And with my funding and yearly allowance dependent on remaining abroad, well, I was forced from my home until I grew up and learned my place."

"That's awful. Miles, I'm so sorry. What your father did to you was reprehensible. And the *London Post*! That newspaper never should have printed something so heinous and slanderous. How dare—"

"I did it." My admission was hardly more than an exhalation, filling the intimate space between us. But it halted her words nonetheless.

I'd never told anyone this, but her defense of me—of the careless man I had been—was something I couldn't tolerate. She needed to know. I'd brought my troubles on myself, in a myriad of ways. Through my recklessness and selfishness, my utter belief that I was above reproach. And from the extremes I'd gone through to antagonize my father.

Endeavoring to strengthen my voice, I confessed, "I planted that article in the *London Post*. Written anonymously and with the help of my friend. I wanted to hurt my father. His self-righteousness, his reputation, and above all his belief in me being anything like him. I just never expected his reaction nor my mother's inability to intervene on my behalf. I got what I deserved, Patty."

With some effort, I met her gaze. It was soft and full of enough sympathy to have me clenching my jaw. "Miles, I don't know that sentencing your child out of your life is the appropriate punishment for acting an indiscriminate youth. Show me a man among the peerage who has not behaved as you've done."

"It's not the same," I said, shaking my head.

"Why not?" Her expression was still even and understanding. "You should be held to a higher standard because of the role your father plays in society? Is that it? Because I'm sure you never asked for that."

"It doesn't matter if I asked for it. It was what was expected of me."

"I know all about expectations," she agreed easily. "All I did was strive to meet mine. And look what it got me—a cold, lonely manor filled with servants who pity me, and a painful separation from my sisters and home. I became the Duchess of Cawthorn because it was expected of me. Patty Bartholomew got left behind. So, you see, it does not matter. Whether we succeed or fail, living for someone else will never bring the happiness we seek. You have to live for yourself, Miles."

She was right, of course. But I could do little more than meet her earnest gaze.

"Can I ask what you hoped to accomplish with the article in the newspaper?"

I looked down at our hands and felt foolish all over again. "I don't know. I just wanted to hurt him. Hurt his reputation, his standing among our peers. I was so sick of their blind faith, their ridiculous obedience to his edicts and teachings. I thought if they saw that his own flesh and blood could ignore the pious charlatan, then perhaps they'd realize what a fraud he actually was."

"I see," Patty said gently.

"Obviously it did not work. His guidance is still sought after. His presence still fashionable in London. I was sent off and he smoothed over the gossip from the actions of his troubled son. I'm sure he claimed I was being counseled while abroad. But the point remained, I was gone. And I couldn't damage his reputation anymore. I was allowed to return this season as long as I maintain good standing. It seems enough time has passed that my misdeeds have been forgotten, or perhaps eclipsed by others like me. Yet my father lectured me upon my arrival as if I was still the same young man who made all those mistakes."

"He doesn't know you at all, Miles." A squeeze of her hand accompanied the statement. "Sometimes we change and no one ever sees it. But we can feel it." Drawing my hand to her chest, she placed my palm directly over her beating heart. "We know it in here. Your father doesn't see the man you've become. He can't. He's too blinded by the past and his own self-importance. He'd rather demean you and minimize you and punish you for all that's happened than truly get to know you as you are now."

Her heart was still pounding beneath my fingertips, and I wanted to be lulled by the rhythm for the rest of my days. "You say that as if it were a bad thing."

"It is. It is his very great loss. He's missing the opportunity to know his son who is intelligent and kind. Funny and charming. He'll have to acknowledge his regrets someday. But, Miles, you've already confronted yours. Don't continue punishing yourself."

For the first time since I admitted the truth of my father, I felt like grinning. So I did. "I'll heed your advice on one condition." Her eyes narrowed and I fought a laugh. "You agree to do the same."

Patty closed her eyes but a smile claimed her lips. "I waltzed right into that, didn't I?"

"You did," I confirmed. "But I think we should both do our best from here on out. And for the rest of this holiday, when your thoughts become intrusive and you feel misplaced guilt and painful reminders, simply seek me out. Give me a signal. Squeeze my hand. Drag me into a cupboard." She laughed, and I smiled at the sound. "Come to me when it all becomes too much. I'll help remind you."

"All right." Her softly spoken reply had me leaning forward to seal the agreement with a kiss.

"All right," I agreed as I nibbled the skin of her bottom lip, tasting the sweetness from the fruit. "I'm still hungry, Your Grace."

"Are you, my lord?" came her breathless reply.

Still facing each other on our sides, Patty pulled back and released my hand. Reaching between us to the plate of fruit and discarded peel, she separated another section of orange from the half remaining. She extended the segment toward me. I gave an enthusiastic bite that had her laughing, the juice from the fruit spraying toward her.

"Oh, no. Let me take care of that." Leaning closer, I set aside the plate and brought my lips to the skin of her neck and shoulders where the shining liquid had landed. I licked and sucked her skin among her lighthearted giggles until her laughter turned to sighs and our skin turned sticky and sweet.

Twelve

MILES

Enduring the holiday with my own family—after spending a fortnight with the Bartholomews—had been a trial in both patience and humility.

While our holiday dinner had been rather sedate with only my mother and father, every night in the Laurel Park dining room had been a fairly boisterous affair. Silas and Emery had battled for the spotlight, and the resulting meals had entertained all those in attendance. Their beloved cook had made all the Bartholomew siblings' favorite dishes to honor and welcome them home. It was quite unlikely that either of my parents even knew what food I preferred.

My father had insisted on scripture readings following our meal, while Emery Ward had tried to convince anyone who would listen that we all should go caroling in the local village. Everyone had groaned at her persistence except me, because the Duchess of Kendrick had announced in an exaggerated whisper what a lovely singing voice Patty possessed. And I found myself very much wanting to hear it.

Our time in the country had been… I didn't have words for how perfect it had been. The servants had been discreet and ignored the fact that they never had to straighten my bed linens, for I spent every night in Patty's suite. In London, I'd been forced to run along home in the wee hours of the morning, to indulge my father and his watchful employees. But at Laurel Park I could make love all night with my duchess. Or I could hold her in my arms while we slept. My actions weren't under the vigilant eye of my father, and the freedom to be with Patty in private was intoxicating and addicting.

However, it was more than simply dreading the company of my father. While I'd been away from London for many years, I could still remember the solitude in growing up a Griffin. My exile had freed me from my cold and unfeeling father for a time, but I'd also been alone and adrift as an outcast, mourning the carefree lifestyle I'd been accustomed to.

I'd grown used to our quiet and dignified household long ago. I had been raised here, after all. Although now the contrast between my father's manor and the lively, chaotic household of Laurel Park was overwhelming. I longed for the comforts of a home—a true home with nosy and opinionated family members who offered love and support unconditionally. Witnessing the Bartholomews' loving—if atypical—household had shone a glaring light on all the deficiencies in my own.

With Patty still in the country, nothing about London would pacify me in my current state, least of all remaining in the presence of the Marquess Salisbury.

Therefore, it was with renewed frustration that I approached the man to see about a townhouse.

Servants were busy removing the garlands from the banister and erasing all evidence of the holiday so recently past.

I frowned as I watched two maids sweep up the needles and debris from the winter foliage. Typically this bout of cleaning in preparation for the new year would require more members of the staff. It was odd to see so few servants set to the task.

Continuing down the corridor to my father's study, I paused and knocked lightly. After a protracted moment, the marquess announced, "Enter."

With a nod of greeting, I sat in the leather armchair I favored while my father remained busy behind his desk.

Without waiting to be acknowledged or addressed, I announced, "Did you instruct our solicitor to prevent me from acquiring property in town?"

He paused in his reading and lowered his spectacles to the desktop. His expression remained unchanged but I could see the subtle disapproval in the tightening of the lined skin around his eyes. "You mean, did I instruct *my* solicitor to prevent you from acquiring property in town?"

I kept my features blank. "I've been turned down from Mayfair to Seven Dials and everywhere in between. Properties mysteriously become unavailable or the original owner decides to move forward with another gentleman. It cannot be a coincidence that I've lost so many opportunities. Why is it that you want to keep me in this house?"

Father produced a handkerchief and began cleaning the lenses of his spectacles. A small chuckle emerged, apropos of nothing. His laughter grew unchecked as my eyes narrowed.

I could count on two hands the number of times I'd heard my father's amusement in my lifetime. He was a staid and practical man with no sense of humor to speak of. There was no place for entertainment or frivolity in his life.

The marquess had been born a second son who'd taken a great interest in the teachings and influence of his father's youngest brother. The man had been a reverend and had died long before I'd been born. But his impact on my father had been absolute. Father had been bound for religious studies at the behest of his uncle-turned-mentor when his elder brother—and the heir to the marquessate —had died in a hunting accident. Though his plans had been derailed, he never abandoned the reverend's teachings and sanctimonious edicts. Now he merely had a different sort of title before his name. The Marquess Salisbury had always valued strict practices, and the fact that he was laughing now with such a cruel edge meant something was very wrong indeed.

Finally managing to speak, he said coolly, "I'd be happy to be rid of you, Basilton, but we simply cannot afford it."

My stony facade gave way to my utter confusion. "What?"

"You'd still be in France if I had the funds to support your exile." He paused in his ministrations to return the cleaned spectacles to his desk. "So, no, you will not be able to let a fashionable townhome in Mayfair for the season. My solicitor knows that your efforts were but a fool's errand."

I was unable to hide my surprise. I didn't relish allowing my father the upper hand, and yet he'd caught me completely unawares. This turn of events was not one I'd ever envisioned. Our holdings and annual income were very comfortable. Unless something drastic had caused this decline, I couldn't imagine the Salisbury title being without wealth.

"Is it a gambling debt?" I asked.

"Of course not," came the incredulous and self-righteous reply.

Naturally the pious man wouldn't be ensnared by such sinful acts. I wanted to roll my eyes. "Then what is it? Why not sell the country estate in Southampton if things are so dire?"

With an imperious tone, he said, "All that remains is this manor. The country home has already been acquired by another, and the Basilton estate and money were used to fund your time abroad."

I laughed, incredulous. "You say that as if I were on holiday. Like I wasn't forcibly turned out and banished from my home."

My father's eyes were cold. "You got exactly what you deserved. I should have sent you to America for your disloyalty and disobedience."

I shook my head, ignoring his vitriol, and bit back the urge to remind him that I was his son—his only son and his heir. "This makes absolutely no sense. How can there be no money? Does Mother know? What are we going to do?"

"I know what *I* am going to do. But I suppose you do have some options before you." From the spiteful gleam in his eye I could tell I would not like where this conversation was going. "Since you've caught yourself such a well-off widow, you could see if she will take you in."

My blood ran cold. Hardening my features, I refused to acknowledge the truth in his words.

"Of course I know you've taken up with the Cawthorn chit. Did you truly think it would escape my notice? Gossip and the late duke seemed to indicate she's barren, so at least you won't end up with a bastard."

I stood so fast that the chair toppled behind me. "Do not speak of her," I forced through gritted teeth. "Do not speak her name."

My warning seemed to amuse my father. "Come now, Basilton. We're grown men."

"You are nothing. Nothing." My clenched jaw could hardly allow the words to pass beyond my lips.

With a scrutinizing glare, he seemed to reach a decision. "I know you are weak of mind and spirit. I've known that since you were a child. Your actions as an adult only further support my opinion. While it's a sinful inclination on your part, I cannot deny that I am unsurprised."

Well, at least he was being honest. I had no illusions of unspoken love and respect from my father. "I appreciate your honest assessment of my failings."

My mocking tone completely eluded him. "It's not just your failings, Basilton. Men everywhere fall victim to the advances of loose women. These harlots lack morals and use their temptations to prey on even good men. It was the ruthless and wicked intent of Lady Wilcox that changed our family's fortune."

Frowning, I attempted to make sense of my father's claims. Lady Wilcox was the widow of the late Earl Wilcox. My father was at least a decade her senior, perhaps two. The Earl and Countess Wilcox had lived at a neighboring estate in Southampton for as long as I could remember. With no children, the title had passed to a distant relative upon the earl's death, and Lady Wilcox had been given the small dowager cottage on the earl's lands. This didn't make sense.

"Lady Wilcox?" I questioned.

The marquess's face screwed up in hatred. "She was a seductress. As vile as Eve in the Garden of Eden. And she claimed to be unable to conceive, but now I am the one paying handsomely for her sinful deception."

Was my father saying…?

"You got Lady Wilcox with child?" I blurted in shock. "And now she's draining you dry to keep the secret?"

When he merely glared, I huffed a disbelieving laugh. The great and admirable Marquess Salisbury, sought for his moral fortitude and ethical teachings, had a bastard, and a mistress who was blackmailing him and likely threatening to expose the truth of his misdeeds. I wanted to laugh in earnest, but there was too much I still didn't know.

"How long has this been going on? Does Mother know?" The thought of my poor mother had all cruel amusement vanishing. She would be devastated by my father's deception.

"Lady Wilcox and her threats have persisted for the better part of six years. And of course your mother is aware of the issue."

The issue. As if we weren't discussing lies and deceit and an innocent child. A child. No longer a baby. And to think he'd been so offended by the gambling accusation. Here he was, a liar and an adulterer, and yet he couldn't seem to muster the appropriate response.

Six years ago. I'd been forced from my home around the same time. I could see now that with the threat of multiple scandals, perhaps my father had been determined to prevent either instance from wounding his reputation. He'd bribed Lady Wilcox and sent me away, all in an attempt at self-preservation.

I suddenly remembered Mother's odd behavior and her hopefulness that I'd simply remain here in residence. She'd known there was no money, and hadn't wanted me to push, to discover the secret.

"The situation should have been well in hand." My father was still speaking as I loomed, fists clenched in anger by my side. "I gave Lady Wilcox the Southampton estate for her to remain in the country, but with the surrender of the infant, she hardly needed such accommodations."

"The surrender of the infant?"

"Yes. That vile woman took care of the problem and sent the girl to an orphanage, but thought to keep her acquisitions and has been demanding more and more from me for the last six years. I've sold what I could and minimized our spending—including your French lodgings and stipend. But that wench has threatened to ruin me." My father's speech ended in snarling disgust.

The girl.

An orphanage.

I had a sister in an orphanage somewhere while there were individuals perfectly capable of raising her. Except they were too beholden to their revenge or their reputations to do the honorable thing. The right thing.

Everyone in London knew that children in those facilities were not better off. Typically malnourished and uncared for, orphans were rarely adopted. They didn't improve their situation as they grew. Most were lucky to survive to adulthood.

I couldn't believe this. I couldn't believe my father had done this.

"Where is she? Where is the girl?"

My father frowned, seemingly confused by the direction of my thoughts. "How should I know?"

I felt my stomach turn over as I approached the desk. "All these years and all of your sanctimonious horseshit. You've done nothing but judge others while turning a blind eye to your own misdeeds. You're a fraud and a charlatan, and you disgust me. I hope your widow takes everything from you. It's exactly what you deserve."

I turned then, unable to look upon my father's face any longer.

"And where does that leave you, Basilton? If I'm ruined, what will become of you and your mother?" His voice followed me through the arched doorway. The threat against my mother had my teeth grinding together in fury.

Leaving the study and walking blindly down the corridor, I passed the same two maids—still erasing signs of the recent holiday. The lack of servants made so much sense now. The marquess had likely reduced the staff by half. How had I not realized?

In truth, I'd avoided this house as much as possible. I found reasons to stay away from my father and this residence. It was entirely plausible that he could turn out most of the servants and I would be none the wiser.

Moving aimlessly toward the front door, I didn't know where I was going nor what I was going to do with what I'd just learned. There were funds I could access. I had assets and investments from my time abroad—of which my father remained unaware. My friend in southern France had a thriving and successful vineyard, of which I was a supporter and partial owner. I could likely sell out my investment, and take my mother and leave this place. There was enough to separate ourselves from the marquess, surely.

Mother.

I couldn't imagine the strain she was under regarding her knowledge of events. I loved my mother. She'd been indulgent, yes. But not only toward me. She'd loved and supported my father for their entire marriage. She'd played peacemaker for much of my adolescence and adulthood, but she respected the Marquess Salisbury and his position in society.

She must be shattered at the knowledge of his deception.

I tried to recall our interactions since my return. I'd assumed the brittle smiles and attempts at levity were due to the stilted relationship between my father and myself. In attributing her odd behavior to my return to London, I'd misread the situation entirely. She'd been covering for him. She'd been—

"Miles, darling. In here."

My mother's voice pulled me from my thoughts and aimless wandering. Turning back to the front parlor, I entered and found her seated near the fireplace with her embroidery. After closing the door, I approached and the smile dropped from her face.

"What's happened?" she inquired, voice not quite steady. "Did you and your father quarrel?"

Sitting stiffly on the small sofa opposite, I ignored her question and said, "Mother, he told me." The conversation with my father was too fresh. I couldn't find my footing to be circumspect.

Placing her hoop aside carefully, she straightened. "Told you what?"

"About the money and Lady Wilcox." After a brief pause, I lowered my voice. "And the baby."

My mother swallowed visibly. "I see."

"Do you, Mother? And yet you remain after his hypocrisy and his betrayal."

"What is it you think I could do, Miles? He is my husband."

I shoved frustrated fingers through my hair. "We could leave. Come with me and we will find a way through this mess. If Lady Wilcox has not been satisfied with the Salisbury fortune thus far, I cannot imagine she ever will be. Father's misdeeds will undoubtedly come to light."

"Be serious. I cannot abandon my husband. I would be ruined. A pariah."

Perching forward on the edge of the settee, I gentled my tone even though on the inside I was screaming my incredulity in the face of her willful avoidance. "I have access to some funds. I just need some time."

But she was already shaking her head, tears gathering and shining in her dark eyes. "I won't leave him. If I can survive learning of these events, I can surely survive when everyone else hears about them."

The devastation I feared but didn't understand was evident now. How someone as kind and warm as my mother could find happiness with that man was nothing short of a miracle. Their match defied all logic, and yet here she remained, steadfast in her loyalty.

"You know, I always wanted more children." The raw pain in her voice cracked my heart. "But he didn't wish to sully his image with an abundance of offspring. And I would have—I would have accepted his child with another. I would have raised her and cared for her as my own. But he wouldn't allow it. So fearful was he of anyone discovering the truth. He said his reputation would be ruined by a bastard."

"And he is right. He spends his days vilifying sinners and preaching against the ungodly. He is a charlatan, Mother. You must see that," I implored as she remained painfully quiet, opinion unchanged. "Do you know what happened to the child? Father claims he does not, but—"

I broke off when I saw the guilt flash across her features, stark compared to her grief.

Leaning forward, I grasped her hands. "Please, Mother. Please tell me what you know."

"What would you do, Miles?"

I opened my mouth, but no words emerged because I did not actually know. I simply needed whatever information she could provide. Somewhere out there was a part of my family, helpless, alone. It made me sick.

Dropping her hands, I stood and paced before the fire. This powerless rage was swelling and I didn't know how to combat it. My father's influence had always seemed vast before, but his offenses were far-reaching in the extreme. His crimes touched so many lives—my mother, this innocent child, all the gullible peers taken in by his hypocrisy.

Finally, I managed, "I do not know what I plan to do. I just know I need to see for myself. Make inquiries. Ensure the girl is safe and cared for."

In the scope of his deception, I realized with dawning comprehension how Patty might interpret my change in circumstance. She'd initiated our arrangement under the belief that I was wealthy—that my family was affluent. That I had no need of her money, and therefore was not a threat in the same way the other men of this town pursued her—doggedly and without honorable intent. She'd noted my comfortable circumstances several times. I feared what this revelation would mean.

I knew that I loved Patty. But she wasn't ready for that revelation. Her marriage to the old duke had broken her convictions, and she was still mending all the pieces. I needed time to make her see—to trust that my devotion was true. That it was something she could rely upon. She needed to know that I would never seek more than her heart.

I would tell her what had transpired with my father when the time was right. First, I needed to inquire after my potential funds and the return on my investment in the French vineyard. Solidify my own means. I would not give up on my mother. And I needed to find out about my father's child…my sister.

Returning to my seat, I faced my mother once more. "Will you tell me what you know?"

She looked down at her hands, gripped so tightly, and spoke without lifting her head, "I made inquiries right after the child was born and turned over. It's been nearly six years now. There's no way to know if she— It was the Kellerman Asylum for Orphans in Bethnal Green."

I let out a relieved breath, and I didn't know why. But something that had been constricting my chest loosened just a bit. "Thank you, Mother. Thank you for telling me."

She nodded absently. "I think— I think I'd like to be alone now, darling."

I tried to meet her gaze, but her attention was very far away. She stood unsteadily. I rose instinctively from my seated position to assist, but before I could reach her, she gained her footing and quit the room. I could understand my mother seeking solitude in her grief. That was natural. But the image of her hand steadying herself on the doorframe as she passed would stay with me for a long time.

Sometimes it was easier to let your heart break behind closed doors.

Thirteen

PATTY

"I have to go."

Miles's whispered confession brought me out of the place I'd been occupying—caught somewhere between restfulness and my large, warm bed.

"Noooo," I groaned before I could catch myself, voice rough from awaiting sleep. It seemed we were destined to repeat this display.

In the nearly two months since we'd been in Hampshire together, Miles had returned to his secret late-night visits to Cawthorn Hall. The threshold we'd crossed in our intimacies in the country had transitioned smoothly back here in London. There was no longer fear from our joining here in my bedchamber. It was as if the panic and dread had been banished finally, once and for all.

Nevertheless, our return had been an adjustment after spending leisurely nights with one another at Laurel Park. We'd been reckless and carried on as if there weren't penalties for our actions. But in the isolated bubble of the guest wing, and with the only consequences being knowing looks from our companions, we'd simply continued being irresponsible, yet happy.

Despite being relegated to secrecy and stolen moments, I couldn't remember ever feeling so joyful—and certainly not in this house.

"Yes, I must," he said into the skin of my neck.

I could feel his body, clothed and ready to depart, pressed against the line of my back, legs cocooned behind my own. The contrast was delicious and made me want to roll over and feel the fabric against the firm flesh of my nipples and between my thighs.

"You know, I'm beginning to think you like me, Your Grace. Perhaps I'm growing on you." The words were softly uttered and mild. He wasn't pressing. This wasn't a declaration or even a demand for honesty. And yet my heart beat a warning in my chest.

Miles might have been teasing just now, but it was true. Something had changed in our time—these months together learning each other's bodies and minds. I hadn't intended to feel more for Miles than reluctant affection and gratitude for his ability to bring me pleasure. However, somewhere along the way I'd softened toward him. I'd become eager for our meetings—more than the bedsport, beyond the arrangement. I longed for his company, his conversation, and his humor. The endless patience he showed me, his kindness—it wore down my sharp edges until I felt like a smooth stone from the creek bed.

Forcing a lightness I did not feel, I replied smoothly, "Yes, I do believe you're growing on me." I felt his mouth touch my neck, and I smiled before I finished, "Like a weed."

The lips lingering on my skin parted to deliver a playful bite that elicited a squeak from me. Still smiling, I rolled to my back as his weight shifted. I watched him rise and carefully tuck the coverlet around my shoulders.

"A weed, am I?" Mock offense was belied by his dimple peeking through. Despite his levity, I sensed something lurking, weighing heavily on Miles in the last month or so. And I could see it now, in the line of his shoulders and the uncertainty in his eyes. Other times, he would be distracted or quiet and thoughtful. And the intensity of his lovemaking left me feeling worshipped and adored.

I didn't know what drove Miles nor the thoughts that sometimes plagued him, but in truth, I wasn't sure it was my place to question him. We had an arrangement that had grown somewhat beyond its borders—much like a weed. But I could not force him to confide in me no matter how I might wish for it. The truth of my desire for his happiness and peace of mind was indeed startling, so much so that I felt frightened to voice it aloud. And so I comforted him with my body and my presence and our very scandalous routine.

My eyelids, heavy with sleep, blinked to keep Miles in focus. "Correct. You're persistent and relentless and I cannot seem to rid you from my garden." He snorted a laugh as my eyes closed of their own volition. "And I'm thorny like a rosebush. We bring out the worst in each other," I mumbled, on the edge of consciousness.

"Do we really, Duchess? Or are you having more fun than you've ever had in your life?"

His question had a smile waking on my face and my eyes opening once more. I feared he did not realize the truth beyond his words.

With his absurdly gorgeous gray-gold gaze twinkling in the dim light of the room, he leaned forward. "Sleep," he whispered, a smile forming the word against my temple.

And the last thing I heard was his soft breath blowing out the final candle, plunging the room into darkness and my languid thoughts into dreams.

~

Visiting Watford House was often a double-edged sword. I felt compelled to attend regularly and enjoyed spending time with the children. But often times, the carriage ride back to Cawthorn Hall would be fraught with guilt and sadness. I'd focused my philanthropic energies to care for and educate orphans in London. But I didn't always feel like my efforts were quite enough.

I knew it wasn't feasible to consider taking in every child who needed a home. Realistically, I knew this. But when I considered my wealth and privilege, it felt like what I was doing was, in fact, not nearly enough.

When a problem was large and insurmountable, even the greatest effort could sometimes feel like merely a drop in the bucket. I tried to remind myself that I was making an impact, changing lives for the better. It might not be enough, but it was something.

A sudden thought struck. I should tell Miles about my relationship with Watford House. He would be…proud, I thought. I didn't particularly know his feelings on children. It had never come up, despite our arrangement. In all the months we'd been intimate, I hadn't had any difficulties with my courses. Perhaps I was barren after all. An admittedly large part of me had hoped that my inability to conceive with the duke had been due to his deficiency, not my own. I supposed now I had my answer.

Regardless, Miles was so charismatic, perhaps he'd enjoy visiting the orphanage with me. The children would adore him, of that I was positive. I'd witnessed his charms firsthand during his time at Laurel Park. Genevieve, despite being a young lady and not a child, had become fast friends with Miles over the holiday in Hampshire. He'd pulled her out of her grief over Julian in a way that Emery and even Silas struggled to do. Miles had gotten her to join us for chilly rides on horseback and meals throughout the day. He inquired after her favorite things and begged her to show him all the best places in the village. I thought she'd enjoyed having someone so unfamiliar who could never be a reminder of Julian —the person who knew her everything. The time and gentle attention Miles had shown my sister had made me grateful and hopeful in equal measure.

I endeavored to push away thoughts of Miles blending in so easily with my family, and be in the moment here and now with the children of Watford House. My feelings for the earl were growing complicated. Here, I was simply the lady in the fancy dresses who came to call.

Currently, I was listening to songs and stories, the children often talking over one another. Francesca was seated right beside me as other children started sharing their improved reading skills and reciting their letters. The little girl held my hand tightly, and I thought about how lovely it was to have watched Franny and so many others grow over the years.

This was my second visit of the new year. Shortly after the lovely holiday in Hampshire with my family, I'd been eager to return to Watford House with the Christmas gifts I usually had for the children. I always enjoyed selecting beautiful dolls and little clothes and storybooks. While it was tradition for me to arrive with two carriage-loads of presents, this year was special in that Mary had asked to accompany me.

I could tell it had still been difficult for her to witness so many children without homes or families, but the visit had gone much better than Mary's first attempt— back before this orphanage in the East End bore the name Watford House. Conditions were vastly improved and all the children were healthy, clean, and well.

Mary had been stiff and unsure upon her arrival, but several curious children had enticed her out of her shell. And once they'd all seen her exuberance, enthusiasm, and penchant for making funny animal sounds, she'd been a very bright light, drawing them all in. I'd caught her wiping a rebellious tear away during our short time in the nursery peeking in on the youngest residents. But she'd recovered admirably and the carriage ride back to Mayfair had been more reflective and less solemn.

However, I was alone today as I made my monthly visit for February. Franny had latched onto my side upon my arrival in the great hall. Her stammer was slightly improved, I noticed. And I could see her visible effort to slow her speech despite her excitement in speaking with me.

I squeezed her tiny hand now and whispered, "I must be going. Your teachers will return for lessons very soon."

"Thank you for my d-d-doll. I love her ever so much," she replied, cuddling her new toy to her chest.

"You are welcome, darling." I smiled, thinking of the doll I'd requested from the toymaker especially for Francesca. Dark hair and a porcelain face with striking hazel eyes painted to match her owner. I was pleased that it brought her comfort and she loved it so.

"All right, children. It is time to return to our classrooms." The teacher stood at the front of the hall and began corralling students. I said goodbye, and they all finally made their way out of the large room—Franny included.

I sat alone on the bench for one more moment before pushing to my feet and straightening my auburn skirts. I could feel the edges of my emotions sharpening, and the guilt I so often experienced beginning to close in.

With a concentrated effort, I made my way back to Mrs. Watford's office to say farewell and collect my things before departing. As I walked along the corridor, I heard a male voice that made me stop in my tracks.

"She would be nearly six years of age—likely with dark hair and perhaps hazel or blue eyes—and part of the previous establishment of the Kellerman Asylum for Orphans."

Shaking myself, I moved closer to the familiar voice, slippers quiet on the hallway runner beneath my feet.

"I understand that you have privacy policies in place, but I just need to know if you have a child here who may fit that description. I don't need to see her or speak to her. I simply want to confirm that she ended up here in this facility after Kellerman's was closed. I'm able to provide the name of the mother of the girl—"

Disbelieving, I approached the doorway to Mrs. Watford's study, the door partially cracked. I could see the back of the man's dark hair and fitted navy-blue suit, and the air froze in my lungs.

"My lord, I understand what you're asking, but I'm afraid that the Watford Home for Children is privately owned now, and I can't simply disclose our records," Mrs. Watford argued.

Why? Why was he here asking about a little girl? What could that possibly mean?

He tried again. "I assure you, I have no nefarious plans. She's—she's my family. I need to know she is cared for."

I must have made a sound at his declaration because Miles turned his attention abruptly away from the headmistress and found my undoubtedly shocked face in the opening of the doorway.

"Patty?" Miles questioned, confused and uncomprehending.

I, however, was understanding more by the second. I took several hurried steps back before turning completely. I abandoned my fur-lined cape and reticule in Mrs. Watford's office and fled through the entryway.

Miles had been inquiring after a child. Here at Watford House. One with *his* dark hair and *his* hazel eyes. I suddenly remembered our conversation about his childhood. His stammer.

Francesca.

Did Miles have a child? Was Franny that child?

I knew what happened when mistresses got with child. If those women were actresses or well-known opera singers, they didn't always wish to be saddled with a titled lord's castoffs. Bastards were often placed in children's asylums and foundling homes. Workhouses also acquired unwanted infants who were the byproducts of disreputable unions between wealthy gentlemen and their mistresses.

Had there been more to the story of Miles's fall from society years ago? Had a baby been the result? One who'd been rejected by her father and surrendered by her mother? Why was Miles looking for her now?

"Patty!" The shout came from behind me as I hurried down the front steps now slick from falling snowflakes. The cold February air was biting and my warm clothes were still back inside the offices of Watford House.

And yet I didn't stop. I couldn't have this conversation right now—not caught out and unprepared. Rationally, I knew Miles didn't owe me anything by way of honesty nor his past. We were but lovers with an arrangement, an understanding. But I'd foolishly allowed myself to misinterpret our relationship these several months. We'd grown closer, shared more than our bodies. The intimacy between us was more somehow. Or so I'd foolishly thought.

I didn't actually know what to think now.

If Miles had a child—sweet, loving Francesca—and had turned her away with no support and no responsibility, I didn't know what that would mean for me. But it made something pierce painfully behind my ribs, and I sucked in a breath.

"Patty!" Miles yelled again, drawing eyes from the sidewalk.

My carriage hadn't been brought around as I'd never called for it. I didn't know where I was going beyond away from this very unexpected encounter and the painful knowledge that I didn't know the Earl of Basilton nearly as well as I'd thought.

I bustled my way around the corner toward the gardens of Watford House and the mews beyond. My skirts swirled the freshly fallen snowflakes as I hurried along the gravel path to reach my carriage. But the effort was futile and I knew it.

"Dammit, Patty. Will you just wait one fucking minute?" His voice was close. And despite the knowledge that I'd have to deal with this uncomfortable conversation, I stopped.

Breathing hard, I thought, *it's time to stop running and face this like you've faced everything else in your life, Patricia. With your head held high and an unaffected air that makes men question the lies they're about to speak.*

I stopped, but I didn't turn. I could hear Miles behind me, breath gusting out as he gathered his resolve or his courage, I didn't know which.

"Will you look at me?"

The urgency had abandoned his tone now that his chase was won. He sounded merely resigned, and that alone would have had my stomach souring in betrayal. But when I turned and saw his pained expression, I knew that whatever Miles had to tell me would not be pleasant.

I didn't want to be right. Not about this. I didn't wish to think that Miles was the kind of man to avoid his responsibilities and allow a child—and her mother—to suffer needlessly. The earl was wealthy. I knew this. It was the impetus in pursuing an arrangement with the man in the first place. He'd never needed my money. But an unexpected child could have used his.

"I can explain." The words were soft, warm breath fogging the tense space separating us.

"So. Explain," I gritted out.

"Don't do that," he admonished. "Don't be the duchess with me right now. We are long since past that."

I took in his frustration—his clenched jaw and the hands fisted at his side—the snowflakes landing lovingly on his long, dark lashes. And I thought, *this is how my heart will break.*

At least it was nice to realize I had one, after all.

Fourteen

MILES

Patty looked untouchable. Every inch the frozen duchess I'd watched from afar in ballrooms across Mayfair. She was shutting me out and closing herself off from me.

For months now, when we were together, she was herself—her true self. Kind and thoughtful, quick to laugh, and affectionate.

The woman before me looked carved from stone and just as cold as the snow gathering on her fair hair. I took in her dark red dress, covered only by her pelisse. Patty's jaw was clenched tight but she was shivering as the snow fell heavily in the garden around us.

Shrugging out of my greatcoat, I moved quickly and draped it over her shoulders before she could object or throw it on the ground. "I know what you heard and how it must sound, but I am not here looking for my own child."

I didn't know why I hadn't already admitted to her the truth of my father and his indiscretions. That was a lie. I knew why. I wasn't ready to bring up the loss of the marquess's fortune—my family's wealth. So I'd held on to the secret of my hidden sister with both fists and refused to confide in anyone as I'd spent the better part of the last month making discreet inquiries and searching for her whereabouts. I'd been told that Kellerman Asylum for Orphans was no more. It had been rebuilt and renamed around the time that my sister would have been surrendered. Writing letters had gotten me nowhere, and for the past fortnight I'd been systematically visiting orphanages, workhouses, and foundling homes in the East End. In most circumstances, my general description hadn't turned up any possible children who could have been sired by the Marquess Salisbury and Lady Wilcox. Thus far, their names had not been found on any records.

Patty had overheard the culmination of my frustration as the headmistress had denied my request repeatedly, once already in writing. So, I'd visited Watford House today and had been…surprised. The facility was warm and inviting, well-furnished and staffed appropriately. The sounds from within were from jovial children, not the crying I'd come to expect from visiting these horrible locations. I had been surprised and suddenly desperate. If my father's daughter had ended up anywhere, I hoped it had been the Watford Home for Children. It seemed the best chance, the most prosperous alternative for her. I'd been desperate to hear the headmistress confirm a child of Lady Wilcox in residence. And my attitude at being denied the only hopeful resolution I could envision had not been suitable.

But beyond my frustration at Mrs. Watford was the utter confusion of seeing Patty—my Patty—here in the first place. What was she doing here?

She was looking at me now, considering my words. But the line of her jaw hadn't softened, and her eyes were accusatory.

"I'm being honest," I attempted, my words swallowed in the stillness. It was nearly silent behind the high walls around the garden. Quiet in the way it only seemed to be when snow fell, flakes thick and slowly drifting all around. With a deep breath, I admitted the truth. "I'm here looking for my father's child. My father's bastard."

Patty's eyes widened, her shock thawing her hard features.

"I found out quite by accident that the marquess fathered a child with his mistress. She surrendered the child to the Kellerman Asylum nearly six years ago. I don't have much more information than that to go on."

Patty's tone was even when she replied. "Watford House stands on the site of Kellerman's. It changed ownership around that time and was dismantled and rebuilt, gutted. New staff and basically everything was changed. The records from before were not well-kept."

I wanted to ask how she knew this, how she came by this information, but she gave a rough shiver inside my black greatcoat.

"Let's get you out of the cold." I recognized her carriage and led her to it.

We settled ourselves on the plush bench seats, Patty sitting opposite as she eyed me cautiously. "What are you hoping to find, Miles? Why are *you* seeking this child and not your father?"

I swallowed against the urge to tell her everything—about the blackmail, the money, all of it. But what emerged from my mouth was, "My father has no interest in bringing his transgressions to light. I merely wanted to find the girl. Perhaps do what I could to ensure she was well."

The words were not enough. But I simply could not bring myself to confess all. After all this time, Patty's reaction today—instant distrust—just proved that she wasn't ready. If she found out about the decline in my circumstances, she'd look at me with cool suspicion once more. I couldn't lose her. I wouldn't.

Patty's eyes softened at my words and she didn't look away from my face as she admitted, "I'm the owner of Watford House."

I frowned, not expecting that.

"During some charity work following the death of my husband, I visited Kellerman's and found the conditions horrific. I directed my philanthropic efforts to creating the Watford Home for Children in its stead. It's really the only orphanage of its kind. The children are more than kept. They're educated and cared for. I've hand-selected the staff and I trust them with all of the children within."

"That's…" My voice trailed off as I considered Patty and her strength and generosity. What it must have cost her emotionally for such a venture, and the possible motivations behind her charitable efforts. "That's amazing, Patty. It's obviously an important part of your life. Knowing your giving nature and soft heart, it's not at all surprising. But why didn't you tell me?"

Her brows pinched. I could see her confusion, the resentment at being questioned, and my heart sank further. But then she looked down at my coat still wrapped around her form and stroked the dark fabric across her lap. "It's odd. While I was visiting the children today, I had a sudden thought that I should tell you about my involvement here. I thought about how good you were with

"Basilton! Thank God you're here. I thought I'd have to be the most charming person at the dinner table." Silas Bartholomew greeted me thus. I heard Lady Mary snort to my left. "Now we can share the load, my good man."

"I shall endeavor to hold up my end of the bargain."

"Yes. By all means, Basilton. Do not let us down in this regard or we shall be subjected to Bartholomew's *charms* all evening long," Mary Lovelace interjected, earning a winning grin from Silas.

I enjoyed the banter about the dinner table. The easiness and informality of a meal shared with family and friends. I'd never known such playful domesticity in my own experience.

Being included in Patty's life—here in London as well as our time at Laurel Park—soothed something scarred and lacking from my own understanding of family. I ached to be more to Patty than the man occupying her bed. This, here and now, was the life I sought. A place by her side and out in the open.

"Lady Mary, I know you are not growing tired of my company. No matter what you insist." Silas eyed Mary playfully over the rim of his wine goblet.

Mary's gaze narrowed. She opened her mouth—likely to fire back a well-placed barb, as was her way—but Patty interrupted.

"All right, children. Enough of your persistent squabbling. Mary, please accept that Silas is endlessly charming. And, Silas, you should accept that Mary is immune to those charms."

Both dinner guests erupted at the same time, speaking over one another and arguing their position. Patty shook her head ruefully as I laughed openly at their antics. Our eyes locked, and I feared everything I was feeling fairly shouted from my chest, carrying down the length of the dining room to land at her feet. All the love and devotion and the fierce happiness I desired from these everyday moments.

And fast on the heels of those emotions came the guilt that I was plagued with. Keeping my circumstances from Patty was wrong. But until I saw the same devotion reflected back at me, I could not be sure that I wouldn't lose her. And I refused to be held accountable and punished for my father's poor choices.

I forced myself to be present and more cautious with my glances. Soon, the footmen arrived with the next course. The food was uninspiring—as was expected from the cook at Cawthorn Hall. No one commented on the undercooked potatoes nor the overcooked fowl. I assumed both Silas and Lady Mary were frequent enough visitors to know not to expect overmuch of the meal. I didn't know if Patty had explained to her brother and her friend her reasons for not sacking the willful cook, but they knew enough to keep their opinions to themselves and eat what was tolerable on their plates.

"Sister, you know Genevieve is quite looking forward to her stay with you next month. That was kind of you to offer."

"Oh, well. I'm…happy to have her, of course." Patty was so uncomfortable with the praise that it was quite adorable.

"And I'm fairly certain she's even excited to see you and not just Basilton over there." Silas raised his goblet in my direction and grinned.

Patty rolled her eyes. "Yes, we all know that Gen and Miles get along famously."

I stage-whispered, "It's because I have the maturity of a sixteen-year-old."

Everyone laughed. But Patty's warm gaze lingered.

During my stay at Laurel Park, I'd done my best to comfort the youngest Bartholomew. I thought she enjoyed having someone about who didn't know Julian. Or better yet, didn't know *her* as she'd been with her missing piece. Memories were often overwhelming and fruitless reminders. Genevieve didn't have merely her own to contend with, but her family's as well. I'd been unknown to the girl, and therefore she'd been unknown to me. There was freedom in that.

As the laughter faded and Silas and Mary dominated the remainder of the dinner conversation, Patty's eyes found mine time and time again. Her smiles came easier, and there was none of the frozen duchess present this evening. I craved this easiness, the mundanity of a meal shared together. I'd grown used to sneaking in through the gardens in the dark of night. But here and now, I felt a part of Patty's life. No longer a dirty little secret.

Fifteen

PATTY

"So, we'll simply tell Francesca that you are my friend and you wanted to visit Watford House."

Miles swallowed nervously, throat bobbing against his patterned cravat. "Will she believe that?"

"Yes, Miles. She will. She's a child. They're painfully honest at times and she would expect nothing less from me."

"All right," he said, fidgeting with the buttons on his waistcoat.

"And it helps that it is also the truth," I remarked dryly, fighting amusement.

"Oh, right. Of course." He still wasn't looking at me. Just standing outside my carriage, staring up at the front steps of the children's home.

"Miles," I groaned. "Look at me." His head jerked in my direction. "You *are* my friend and you do simply want to visit Watford House."

"I know." He straightened, wiping a hand along his dark brow. "I know that."

I simply waited as his gaze darted around our surroundings. It wasn't snowing like it had been last week on these very same steps, but it was still cold and damp.

"I'm just nervous, Patty. I feel mad. I want her to like me, but I also don't want to impose myself upon her life here. I don't want her to ever question our relationship."

My frown was immediate and severe. "Why?"

His fidgeting stopped and he lowered his voice while meeting my gaze. "Because I don't want her to ever consider her parentage and why someone somewhere didn't want her."

"Oh, Miles." My heart ached. He was so very conflicted. And that just made me angry because his heartless father was warm in his manor, feeling no worse for wear. But here was his son, fretting and anxious in the East End while he prepared to meet his sister.

Following the discovery of Miles at Watford House a week ago, I'd returned the next day with a special request to any information we had on Francesca's history. Mrs. Watford had been very confused, but I'd never asked for such privileges, nor had I needed to. Francesca had been turned over to the Kellerman Asylum shortly after her birth. I'd purchased and transitioned the property the very same month. But despite the brevity of the Kellerman records, her mother and father had both been listed on all documentation.

Once I'd confirmed my findings, I'd told Miles. It was quite different to suspect something as opposed to knowing it and seeing the proof. I thought momentarily of Francesca's brilliant eyes, and realized I'd never been waiting on confirmation from any documents.

Miles had been both uneasy and relieved. At least he now knew that Franny had been cared for far better than most orphans in London. But the knowledge obviously didn't sit well with him. He'd confessed he'd wanted more for the girl. He felt compelled as her family to see her provided for. He wanted to demand that the marquess take her in. But knowing how he'd been raised himself, I was sure Miles felt conflicted on that front as well.

I didn't know how Franny's story would end, but I had an inkling, a feeling that I needed to explore after today's visit. I was eager to see Miles with Francesca. So I just kept reassuring him that we'd figure this out, and would take things one step at a time.

And now I was patiently waiting for him to stop perspiring on the steps of the building, and go meet his sister.

Following a deep breath, he said, "All right. I'm ready."

So, very gently, I placed my hand in the crook of his elbow and led him up the first step. Miles followed and soon we'd reached the front doors. Then the foyer. After relinquishing our warmer clothing items to the main floor maid, Dara, I guided Miles toward the great hall which currently sat empty. I'd purposely brought Miles during lessons so he wouldn't be overwhelmed by all the children upon our arrival. We'd be able to peek in on the classes taking place, and when the younger students were released for tea, we could join Francesca with hopefully very little fanfare and curious glances.

"I didn't see this part of the property when I spoke with Mrs. Watford," Miles whispered quietly near my ear.

I fought a shiver at his proximity. "The home was built from practically the ground up. As stages of construction were complete, we transitioned the children over as space became available. I had a very clear vision for Watford House and was fortunate to find an architect and builder to bring that vision to life."

He nodded as his gaze roamed the large space with high ceilings and long tables to seat all the children and staff. "And there are classrooms and nurseries?"

"Yes, and governesses who provide education in reading and writing, arithmetic, and some music lessons. If certain young ladies take an interest in French or Italian, I try to bring in tutors. Those language skills can be beneficial in finding positions for them later on."

We were closing in on the corridor on the far side of the great hall that led to the instruction rooms, but Miles stopped abruptly. "But what sort of future can Francesca really have? Will she be apprenticed to—some—some master? Doing what? It's not right that her future should be thus. She deserves a family. A dowry. Comfort. I don't know if I can do this."

He spun as if to escape but his boots remained firmly planted as he faced away from me, determination warring with the desire to run.

"How do you bear it, Patty? I haven't even seen her yet, and already— I— I— don't know if my heart can manage."

Approaching slowly, I fitted my small hand in his and rested my chin atop his shoulder. Gentling my voice, I did my best to reassure him. I'd been where he was now. I'd felt these feelings. Wanting only to help, to save everyone in my path. "I bear it because I must. I cannot save every orphan in this city. But the ones in my care—at Watford House—will know better lives. They'll apprentice to good masters. They'll be educated. They'll have my support and connections. Some may be companions or maids in high-ranking houses. The men will learn trades and have homes and families. These children will know love."

Miles hung his head as he considered my words. And then, finally, he squeezed my hand and turned to face me. With no warning nor preamble, his gloved hand cradled my jaw and he kissed me. It wasn't wild or passionate. He didn't claim with his lips. But the surety in his kiss nearly undid me, as if we already belonged.

It was patient and kind. It was a kiss of love.

And I wasn't panicking at the thought.

When he pulled away, Miles simply took in my expression before saying, "That's some heart you've got there, Duchess."

I didn't know how to respond to the pride I saw shining in his eyes. So I simply replied, "Come, I want to show you everything."

His smile was crooked and pleased, and I felt something quite dangerous tighten in my chest. Something that felt like more than an arrangement. More than being lovers hidden away.

Now was not the time to examine these intrusive thoughts, these inconvenient feelings.

As I led Miles out of the main hall and down the corridor, the sounds of children began to bring the building to life. There was singing from an adjacent hallway, a violin being attempted from somewhere farther down, and the angry wails from a small babe. We passed the nursery first and I could see the nursemaid swaying gently with the red-faced infant. Her soft shushing had the child quieting and clutching a fistful of her apron as they danced around the room. Several other babies were napping in their beds while a tiny girl toddled on unsteady legs. The fair-haired child wobbled over to the nursemaid and clasped her skirts happily while the woman praised the girl for walking so well.

The exchange—while warm and exactly what I wanted for this children's home—sent a wave of longing so deep and wide I pressed a hand to my chest.

Stepping smoothly away from the doorway, I continued down the hallway in the direction of Francesca's classroom. Miles turned wide and expectant eyes on every room we passed. Soon we discovered young Turner—a boy of nine—in the music room. The sounds of his violin lesson had Miles and I sharing a genuine smile. Leaving the boy, we turned a corner. Slowly, I approached a partially closed door.

Miles stepped up beside me, casting a wary glance my way. I offered a small, reassuring smile as we took in the scene. The door stood ajar at the rear of the classroom. All the students at their tables—eight young children in all—faced forward with their backs to us. I found Franny easily enough. Her long hair had been plaited back and she sat up eagerly, watching the instructor at the head of the classroom.

"Now, class, shall we practice writing our alphab—" The governess broke off as she noticed our presence in the entryway.

The students turned, curious about the interruption, and I felt Miles stiffen beside me.

"D-duchess!" Francesca fairly shouted and leapt from her seat in youthful exuberance. The other children said hello and started speaking over one another, but remained seated. Franny flung her little arms around my skirts. I could not help but smile down at her cherubic face. "You don't normally visit again so soon."

"Well, I do not wish to disrupt your studies, my dear, but I've brought a friend with me to tour Watford House." I paused to peer over at Miles. If I thought he'd be slow to recognize his own kin, I should not have worried. By the look of wonder on his face, I could tell immediately that he'd identified his sister whose attention was still focused on me. "Now run along back to your teacher. I will see you shortly for tea, yes?"

"Yes, Your Grace," Franny said sweetly before returning to her seat.

I apologized for our interruption and returned to the hallway. Miles flattened his back to the wall as the governess resumed her instruction, the children settled once more. He was breathing roughly, gaze unfocused. I could not read his expression. It could very well be overwhelming panic.

Positioning myself before him, I whispered, "Are you all right?" When he didn't respond or take note of my presence, I cupped his cheeks gently. "Miles?"

His brilliant hazel eyes—more mossy gold in this moment—snapped to my face. "That was her," he breathed. Not a question.

I smiled and nodded, though he required no confirmation. He'd seen and heard Francesca for himself. There was no denial in his tone, simply acceptance. My heart beat faster at the implication, knowing and brave in a way I would have to consider later. "Shall we stay for tea and visit with her and the other children? Do you feel ready for that?"

His jaw moved in my palms as he nodded his acquiescence. "I'm afraid I'll frighten her with my curiosity. I don't know how to look at her any other way. As if she's not the most wonderful thing I've ever seen."

My breath caught at his sincerity and awe. I understood exactly what he meant. He feared his heart would give him away.

I found I was struggling with the same concern. I only hoped Miles was too engrossed in this moment and distracted by thoughts of his sister to realize I must be staring at him with the same raw longing and sense of wonder. *As if he is the most wonderful thing I've ever seen.*

Willing away these untidy emotions, I sought to reassure him—and myself as well. "Children are rather self-involved. I doubt she'll read too much into your expression nor your questions. She'll be so focused on showing you everything and talking to you."

Miles huffed a laugh. "That sounds about right."

Smiling, I released his jaw and made to step away, but he quickly snagged my hands in his, squeezing gently.

"Thank you, Patty. Thank you for bringing me here. Thank you for letting me meet her."

"Of course," I replied easily, ignoring the thoughts desperate to escape. *Tell him. Tell him you care for him. Tell him he could have everything.* Driving away that bit of lunacy, I settled on, "It will all work out. She will adore you."

A short while later we were settled in the main hall with all the children, save those in the nursery. Francesca sat close beside me with her doll in her arms, while Miles was seated opposite.

"You can hold her if you are very careful, my lord." Franny's tone was so serious that I fought a smile.

Miles nodded solemnly and held out both hands across the tabletop. "I swear it. I shall take the utmost care, Miss Franny."

She smiled, enjoying the attention. "Don't forget to support her head, if you please."

I covered my mouth in an effort to smother a laugh. She'd been told the very same from the nursemaids when she asked to hold the infants.

Finally, after Miles's seriously uttered, "Of course," Francesca extended the doll carefully into his waiting arms. The little girl nodded approvingly as he cradled the doll to his chest. "Am I doing well, do you think?" he asked before shooting me a wink. He'd grown calmer and more confident as teatime progressed.

"Yes, my lord. She's very content. Do you have children of your own?"

The girl's abrupt question had Miles's eyes widening as I fought another laugh. He clearly did not realize how honest and invasive children could be. I bit my lip as he floundered.

"Well— I— No, I do not."

His uncomfortable gaze flitted to me briefly, and suddenly I wasn't fighting amusement any longer. Something unfurled within. Something wanting and desperate. But I was determined to ignore these inconvenient feelings at present. Being here—at Watford House, with both Miles and Franny—was making me wish for things. I needed time to sort out my feelings on the future, and it certainly did not help to have Miles looking at me the way he was. As if he, too, was considering where we went from here.

"Pity," Franny replied, oblivious to the awkwardness her question had wrought. "You'd make a lovely father, I'm sure."

"Thank you, Francesca. That's a rather fine compliment," Miles replied before his gaze touched mine once more. "Who knows what the future will bring?"

duchess. And then others closed ranks and we danced. It was both the shortest and longest waltz in the history of the ballroom. The moment stretched and expanded with every twirl and step. She felt warm and soft beneath my hands.

We neither spoke nor hardly looked away from one another. I feared I was breathless for more reasons than one. And finally, in a blink, it was over. The musicians concluded, the dancers bowed, and still we stood.

"Lord Basilton, would you escort me from the dance floor?"

I nodded as Patty placed her hand on my arm. Together we made our way back to Lady Mary, the crowd of revelers parting easily before us.

"Good evening, Lord Basilton. What a fine event this is turning out to be." Mary's eyes glowed with a touch of mischief that likely would never abate, but also something genuine and warm shone from those brown depths.

Clearing my throat, I finally returned her greeting. "Good evening, Lady Mary. I find that I quite agree with you."

Patty's voice came quiet and uncertain from my side. "Are you all right? Should I have not—"

"No," I interrupted quickly. "You should have. I'm glad you did." I smiled and Patty's own relief reflected back at me. "I'm sorry I made you doubt your actions. I was just surprised." Lowering my voice, I attempted to explain my odd behavior this week. "I apologize for pulling away after all that has happened. I have some other things I need to tell you, but I've felt so powerless. It's hard to put into words." I needed to figure this mess out with my father. I needed a plan. And if I truly wanted Patty to be my partner, I needed to be honest with her about everything. About the money and what I actually wanted. Not this arrangement, but a life together. "Can we talk? Tonight? I can come to you."

"Of course," Patty answered easily. Her concern was palpable. "I think we should talk. I've been thinking, and I believe I have an answer to our—"

"Patty! Your dear sister is here!" Mary's overly loud voice drew our attention away from the intimate conversation we'd been on the verge of having in a very nosy ballroom. While frustrating, Patty would probably be grateful for the interruption.

Stepping away smoothly, Patty took in the many gazes pointed our way before looking to Mary. Her smile was brittle, but her reply was even. "You're right. The Duke and Duchess of Kendrick have arrived."

"Your heartfelt declarations will have to wait until everyone in Mayfair isn't staring at you, Patricia," Mary hissed as she looped her arm through her friend's. And then at a normal volume, she said, "Please excuse us, my lord. We'll return shortly after greeting the duchess's close relations."

"Yes, of course." I bowed as the ladies bustled toward the opposite side of the ballroom where the hosts for the evening's festivities were welcoming Augustus and Emery.

After a long exhale, I spun back to face the ballroom and came boot to boot with Thomas Faulk quite unexpectedly.

"Ho, Basilton! I must say I am surprised to see you out this evening."

My eyes narrowed at the smug expression the man wore like a dinner jacket—a bit tight across the top. "Your family throws a lovely party, Finnigan. Why should I be disinclined to attend?"

The man's dark eyes sparked, defiant and cruel. I could not for the life of me recall why we'd ever been friendly. "Well, if my father was approaching close supporters looking for a loan, I believe I'd avoid drinking in their homes for the evening."

"What?" The question burst out, incredulous and quite against my will.

"Come now, Basil. You didn't know what Salisbury has been about? I find that rather hard to believe. Don't you, Caldwell?" As Viscount Finnigan spoke, the circling and eavesdropping vultures descended. Ebenezer Petty approached with Pritchard and Edgemoore. A half dozen other gentlemen gathered to hear my response. But I didn't know what to say.

If my father was desperate enough to approach his acquaintances for loans, then he was determined to keep Lady Wilcox at bay. And if he'd been smart enough to seek out supporters with pockets bigger than their mouths, then he might have met his ill-advised goal. Unfortunately for the Marquess Salisbury, these gentlemen were anything but discreet. There was no honor among gold diggers, and word had obviously spread regarding my father's decline. But they didn't know about Francesca, or Finnigan would have led with that juicy bit of gossip.

"I can't say that the marquess and I are on good terms, Finnigan. Surely you recall?" I could feel sweat gathering under my cravat. Where was Patty? I needed to speak to her and stop wasting time here with these imbeciles.

"Oh, I do," the viscount agreed easily with a smile. "But I can't help but think if he'd known you'd landed the Duchess of Cawthorn, he wouldn't have been asking my father in the first place. That purse could keep him flush for the rest of his life. And yours too, I'd wager."

As if I'd found great humor in Thomas's pithy remark, I attempted to speak over their loud, braying laughter. "We danced, gentlemen. You presume too much." Panic suddenly tightened my voice.

"Say!" Lord Caldwell spoke over me. "I think that means Basilton won the bet, gents. Who would have thought after all these months that Basil would stroll in fresh from France and woo the ice queen out from under us? Don't worry, sir, once your engagement is announced, we shall all pay up. Sounds like you could use the scratch."

Their laughter continued as more eyes turned our direction.

I shook my head. The heat was gathering all along my back. I could feel the unease spreading.

Oh, Christ. The idiotic bet from the beginning of the season when I didn't give a fig what they were going on about. It had been the interference of these men that had ruined that first dance with Patty. The misunderstanding that had led to our rocky start.

The Gaggle was closing in despite my protestations. They were slapping my back and pumping my hand even as I stepped away, attempting to extract myself and put as much distance as possible between myself and these men.

As I stumbled back, the room grew quiet save for the musicians still hard at work near the center of the dance floor. I couldn't tell if anyone was even dancing. The prickling unease flared back to life as I spun around and came face-to-face with the frozen glare of Patricia Henney.

She was flanked by a wide-eyed and disbelieving Mary Lovelace and a fierce-looking Emery Ward. My frantic gaze bounced around to those assembled. Augustus gave me a subtle shake of his head, what I presumed was a silent warning to avoid overacting and causing a scene.

My eyes came back to Patty's frosty blue stare, and it was clear from her expression that she'd heard it all. My father's need for money, the back-slapping congratulations on landing the duchess, and the ludicrous bet. All of it coming back to bite me in the arse.

"Patty," I attempted, voice calm even as my heart raced out of control in my chest. Fear and panic welled dangerously along the banks of my resolve.

One imperious blond brow rose, dismissing me and challenging me at the same time. She was the duchess through and through. And I was the gutter trash upon her elegant slipper.

Her frosty glare lifted as she scanned the room and those witnessing this carriage crash of epic proportions. With a final dismissive glance, Patty turned and glided gracefully from the ballroom, her sister and her friend close behind. Kendrick gave me a pleading look before he, too, turned and joined their departing forms.

I could explain this. I knew well enough to know that confronting her now and drawing even more attention to our scandalous behavior would not be well-received. Patty had heard the worst, the very things that would make her doubt me and my honesty. But I could fix this.

I took a deep breath and let it out slowly. Even as my stomach hollowed out and my hands began to shake, I still believed I could explain this horrible misunderstanding compounded by abysmal timing. Patty knew me. She knew my heart. I was not like these fortune-seeking fools.

Yes, she'd been unaware of my troubling financials. That was an idiotic secret to have kept. But I could explain.

My breath was coming in pants. I needed to get out of this room before I murdered these men who'd ruined things yet again.

No, that wasn't accurate. I'd omitted the truth from Patty. I needed to own up to my mistakes and shortcomings. I should have told her the truth when I had the chance, as soon as I realized I was without funds. I'd let fear influence me and it could very well destroy everything.

My legs started moving before I'd actively decided. I would go to Cawthorn Hall. I would talk to her. I would not approach in public, nor would I make a spectacle. I would be calm and rational. Patty would see reason.

Seventeen

MILES

"So, what's the plan, then?"

I squinted through bleary eyes to make out the voice. Optimistic, hopeful, painfully cheerful. Must be... I squinted harder.

"How drunk are you?"

Ah, yes. Silas Bartholomew.

I was saved from answering the man's question by Augustus Ward—ever the gentleman, and hardly as drunk as Daly and myself.

"He is quite drunk, Silas." Kendrick's tone was unruffled. He had no reason to be ruffled, honestly. Daly and I had been top-notch drunkards. Hardly caused a scene at all.

We'd been in a private room at the club for most of the night. I couldn't remember why, but I assumed Kendrick was here to keep us alive as Daly and I drowned our respective sorrows.

And now Bartholomew was here and a fresh wave of hurt cascaded as I thought of his sister. They shared a similar bone structure. Regal and imposing. Elegant and classical.

I nodded at his reassurance, eyes following the words across the page.

"I may add a few flourishes to the writing, increase the drama before the big reveal."

"Of course," I agreed absently.

"So the final article may change—"

"George, I trust you. Just let me read it, will you?"

My friend placed a hand over his mouth and leaned back in his chair, crossing one leg over the other. "Right," he mumbled. "Apologies."

I raised a brow at him but went back to scrutinizing the paper.

Minutes later, after reading the very last line, my eyes flicked up to George who still held a hand over his mouth. "It's perfect."

His breath rushed out, making a rude sound against his palm before he recovered. "Thank God."

Standing stiffly, I noted the late hour on my pocket watch. "When will you run it? I need a few days to set the rest of my affairs in order."

George stood as well. "Sunday, I should think. That should give us both enough time."

Three days. I could last three more days.

I nodded, reaching out a hand. "I thank you for your friendship, George. And your willingness to help me out of a tight spot once again."

"Of course, Bas. I know it was your idea, but this will sell a lot of papers. The downfall of the Marquess Salisbury. Every household from Maida Vale to Seven Dials will have a copy. I should be thanking you."

We said our farewells and I left Fleet Street, quiet for once at such a late hour. I hailed a hack and moved forward with the next part of the plan, and hopefully the rest of my life.

I was ready to leave indecision behind and be the man I knew I could be. A suitable partner to Patty. One who valued her input and didn't diminish her even in the face of my own weakness. I was prepared to be a source of love and security for my sister. Francesca deserved more than the hand she'd been dealt. She deserved every happiness from a doting and reliable elder brother. And I could envision the future, as a family. I was determined to make it a reality.

However, the following morning, when I arrived in the East End, Mrs. Watford told me quite plainly that Francesca was no longer a resident of the Watford Home for Children.

Eighteen

PATTY

... It has come to our attention, here at The London Post, that the Marquess Salisbury is not at all what he seems. This simple man, by all appearances devout in his faith and strict in his teachings, has more than skeletons in his closet. This reporter has it on very good authority that the marquess has long held a mistress in the country, and a child—unclaimed and abandoned—in a London orphanage. The news of the marquess's indiscretions is doubly appalling, especially for a man such as himself who holds others to such exacting standards.

When I consulted my source for the information in this article, he said he no longer wished to remain anonymous. The marquess's own son, Miles Griffin, the Earl of Basilton, came forward to set the record straight and enlighten those followers taken in by his scheming father. "The supporters of the Marquess Salisbury shouldn't be lied to any longer. A man who ignores his own principles is not a man who deserves praise and accolades. Continuing to allow Salisbury's influence in our homes and over our peers does a disservice to all who heed his lies. Someone once told me that you should be honest. Even when it could ruin everything. I can no longer keep my father's secrets, for his misdeeds and misconceptions have hurt far too many people already."

There you have it. The readers of the London Post *deserve better than the lies of a charlatan. This establishment has long since revered and praised the Marquess Salisbury for his religious teachings and purity of heart and mind. But after his dastardly truth has been revealed, our position has altered dramatically, and we can no longer support this scandalous injustice.*

I forced my hand to steady as I folded the newspaper and placed it facedown on the seat beside me. The words were the same no matter how many times I'd reread them. The article was three days old, but I hadn't yet forced myself to throw the newsprint out.

The truth isn't there for when it's merely convenient. Be honest, even when it's hard. When it could ruin everything.

"Your Grace, may I have some more bacon?" Francesca's eager question returned my attention to the dining room from which it had strayed. The little girl was perched on a paisley velvet throw pillow in order to reach the table more effectively. The upper portion of her dark hair was styled away from her sweet face.

"Of course, Franny. You may have as much bacon as you wish." I moved the platter within her reach. "And you can call me Patty, dear."

"S-sorry, I forgot." She smiled a gap-toothed smile that made my heart squeeze. Francesca's hazel eyes were bright as she retrieved her bacon and gathered another slice of bread with marmalade.

Would those eyes be a constant reminder?

Miles.

What in the bloody hell had he done?

That article left nothing to chance. There had been no subtlety about it. He had laid out the Marquess Salisbury's crimes quite plainly and identified himself as the informant.

Be honest, even when it's hard.

Miles had ruined his father. He'd obliterated the man's reputation. There was no coming back from that article, no matter how the marquess might try to spin it. He would not be welcome in any home of the peerage ever again. Not only had Miles brought to light the crimes of his father, he'd played on the pride of all those who followed his teachings. He'd made a fool of anyone who'd sung Salisbury's praises, ensuring there would be none remaining. The aristocracy would be scrambling to put distance between themselves and the marquess, attempting to downplay any association they might have had.

Miles's mother had not been mentioned, and I was sure that was purposeful. I hoped the marchioness was all right.

When it could ruin everything.

God, Miles. I hoped he knew what he was doing.

What was I saying? I hardly knew what I was doing.

I'd accepted Francesca as my ward and brought her to live with me, which was practically unheard of as she was not my relation. But I wasn't concerned about that. As Emery had reminded me, I was a wealthy, widowed duchess. I could get away with rather a lot.

I cared for the girl. We'd always had a special bond. I'd watched her grow from a small babe.

And despite how things had gone with Miles, I knew he was desperate for the child to have a home and a family. Perhaps his pride wouldn't allow him to ask for my money or my assistance. I couldn't know his reasons for holding tightly to his secrets for so long. But I could help Francesca. Maybe that would be enough for Miles.

Part of me hoped it wasn't. Not nearly enough.

I didn't know what Miles had planned for the future, for himself or Francesca. But the article printed in the *London Post* showed me that he was not without resolve. And he'd obviously taken my words very much to heart. He wasn't going to let his father win this time. And the honesty and humility he displayed in coming forward with the truth was not lost on me.

It had to mean something, did it not?

Focusing my attention back on Franny, I gave her a bright smile. "Very soon, Lady Mary and my sister Emery will be joining us. Would you like to go shopping with them? Perhaps we could find some pretty ribbons, if you like. Or a nice new bonnet?"

The child practically bounced in her seat in her excitement. "Oh, yes, please, Your Gr— Patty," she corrected with a shy smile. "I would like that very much."

Francesca was settling in nicely here at Cawthorn Hall in the last week or so. I'd had a room made up for her and prepared the staff beforehand. I'd finally had the necessary talk I'd been avoiding with Mrs. Bunce, our cook. She'd been instructed to improve her attitude and her meals for the newest member of our household or she'd be out of a job. It seemed I had trouble standing up for myself with the old woman, but when it came to championing Francesca, I'd found the motivation quite easily.

I'd written to my mother, who did not understand what had compelled me to make such a decision, but she would be arriving from Hampshire in the upcoming week to meet Franny. My father and Genevieve would be accompanying her as well.

We were learning our way together—Francesca and I. And I was more than likely smothering the girl with my attention, but I never wanted her to feel lonely in this large home. I'd hired a governess to oversee her education for a portion of the day, but I wanted to take my meals with Franny, and show her all around London. I was desperate to give her the life she deserved. The one Miles had wanted for her.

And perhaps someday Miles would be in a position where he could want this life for himself as well. I wasn't angry with him. Not really. Not anymore. I'd been more hurt than anything. But I hadn't been lying when I said I did not wish for a repeat performance of my marriage to Cawthorn. I wanted a partner who valued my opinions and sought my counsel.

Miles needed to find his truth and live it. And from the article printed recently, perhaps he was on his way to finding it.

I'd been bound to my choices for a very long time. I hoped that Miles could find freedom in his.

"Your Grace." Mr. Pitch's voice at the entry of the dining room drew my attention from my thoughts. "Your visitors are here. Shall I show them to the formal receiving room while you and Miss Francesca finish your meal?"

"Feel free to show them in here, Mr. Pitch." Emery and Franny could bond over their shared love of bacon.

Francesca stared wide-eyed at the flurry of activity and introductions. She recalled Mary from her visit to Watford House earlier in the year. My friend greeted the child warmly and passed her a wrapped parcel that she called a welcome gift. Augustus was a calming contrast to Emery's eager excitement. My sister made herself at home right beside Francesca and the two became fast friends straight away, chatting amiably and discussing their favorite dishes.

Smiling at the domestic scene before me, it took a moment before I noticed the lingering form just beyond the archway to the dining room. Miles stood there, looking uneasy and nervous.

I'd stood before I realized my intention, my chair making an obtrusive scraping sound that drew the attention of those in the room.

"If you'll excuse me," I murmured.

"Take all the time you need," my sister replied, smiling broadly. "I'm going to show Francesca how to make my famous bacon and jam sandwiches."

"Please no, Emery," Augustus groaned. "The only thing they are famous for is making you ill when you were nine and ate four of them."

I didn't quite hear my sister's response nor the playful bickering that followed because I was too focused on the man hovering uncomfortably near the doorway. His dark hair had been thoroughly worked over by nervous fingers. He looked unsure, and so unlike his typically confident and charming self that I could hardly stand it.

"I'm sorry, I know I should not be here. But after everything with…" Miles trailed off as I grasped his hand in mine and led him down the corridor.

Moving quickly toward the short entryway at the rear garden entrance, I threw open the door and dragged Miles into the bright morning sunlight. Squeezing his fingers, interlaced with my own, I led him along the stone pavers toward the flower beds.

I settled us on a sturdy sun-warmed bench to one side of the main path.

"Are you all right?" I asked before any awkward silence had the chance to descend. "I saw the article. Your poor mother. Francesca and I have been rather secluded here and I haven't heard—"

My words were cut off as Miles leaned forward and embraced me, arms wrapping tightly around my middle, bringing me flush against him. I breathed out a sigh as I returned his hold, my own arms banding about his shoulders and clutching him back just as securely.

"I've missed you so much. I'm sorry, Patty." He breathed the apology into the skin of my neck, his heat and proximity making gooseflesh rise. "I'm sorry for everything. I should have been honest with you. But I'm learning, I swear it."

"I know." I laughed, pulling back slightly, needing to see his face in the bright light of this very new day. Emotion threatened, but this was a conversation we desperately needed to have. "I saw the article. I read your words. I read *my* words."

His expression remained serious. "After I set things in motion with the *London Post*, I went to get Franny. But I was too late. And then I found out she was here, with you. And I didn't dare to hope, but I could not stop myself. I would have come sooner, but I've been dealing with the fallout from the article."

"What has happened?" I asked, honestly curious to hear.

Miles let out a long breath. "So much, Patty. You wouldn't believe. The marquess has lost all of his supporters. They've cut off all their funding and connections. He had more loans than my mother or I ever knew about. He's left. Gone with Lady Wilcox, of all people. They've run off to America." I gasped at the revelation. "I suppose she has more than enough money to see them settled across the Atlantic, and my father is smart enough to hitch himself to a well-appointed wagon."

The relief I felt was sharp. I hadn't realized it until this moment, but I'd been somewhat afraid that Salisbury or Lady Wilcox herself would cause trouble for Francesca. I never wanted her to know of her past. I feared her mother or father would only seek to use her to their advantage. Yet Miles had delivered wonderful news regarding the marquess and his mistress.

"They are gone. And no longer your concern. Nor do they pose a looming threat to Francesca. That is truly what matters. Your mother. How is she?" I reached over and grasped his nervous hands, stopping them from combing through his messy hair again.

"She's upset, of course," he said, frowning. "But I told her about meeting Francesca, and she essentially chose us. We've sold the Salisbury London residence, and found my mother a townhome of her own. I think she could use a bit of space while the gossip dies down."

I squeezed his hands, trying to offer comfort. "That is what London is good for. There will be a fresh scandal any day now, and eventually your mother will be able to move on with her life. It may not look as it did before, but she'll have your support, and that will make all the difference."

"I did hear a bit of gossip, actually," Miles said with searching eyes. The sunlight made them glow golden.

"Oh, really?" I replied, raising a playful brow as he watched me closely. "What was that?"

"That the Duchess of Cawthorn has taken on a ward rather unexpectedly, and she's bought out nearly every toymaker in the city."

I scoffed, but admitted, "There might be some truth in that."

There was so much hope in his hazel eyes, Miles was practically brimming over with it. "Why, Patty?" The question was part desperate anticipation and the rest fearful wonder.

Taking in our beautiful surroundings, I searched for honesty and courage among the pink and white blooms. I found I could not force him to wait any longer. "If you can be honest, then so should I," I replied, meeting his expectant gaze. "I love you, Miles. And I want a family with you. It won't be traditional, of course. A strange and broken family that likely will not be accepted beyond our novelty. But you were right about Franny deserving more. Being owed a family. And that could be us, if you want it to be."

And suddenly I was back in his arms, crushed by the weight of his joy as he stood and spun me around. When he paused, warm lips found mine, passionate in their relief.

"I love you, Patty." Another kiss, pressed tenderly to my forehead as he set me down gently. Cradling my cheeks, he admitted, "I've loved you for so long. I want to marry you and raise Francesca together. I promise to be a worthy partner in all things. We will make each other so damn happy, Duchess. I know it."

I smiled back, happy in the knowledge that there was a future for us after all. And while it might not have been the one I'd envisioned for myself all those years ago, it was infinitely better. It would be loud and messy and full of a life worth living.

Miles kissed me once more, sweetly on the lips, before looking over my head to our surroundings.

I turned, attempting to find whatever had distracted him. "What is it?"

He smiled, dimple deep and lovely. "This is quite the garden. I've only ever seen it in the dark."

I laughed, considering how very unexpected our journey had been. From an arrangement that had Miles sneaking in the garden entrance to a future, happy and bright. "Well, perhaps I can take you on a tour, my lord."

"I would enjoy taking a turn about the grounds with you, Your Grace. Especially if there is a secluded corner you'd like to show me."

My grin felt enormous on my face. I held out my arm in order to be a proper escort and Miles laughed loudly, gamely slipping his hand in the bend of my elbow.

"Are you ready?" I asked, suddenly breathless with anticipation, the familiar buzz beneath my skin at his nearness never abating. Not once in all our time together.

His smile gentled as he searched my face before saying easily, "I am, Duchess. I'm ready for all of it."

As we strolled through the glorious spring day and the grounds of Cawthorn Hall, I could not help but think…

Our love had taken the unpredictable route, but now it lived boldly in the light.

Nineteen

MILES

Several months later

"What about this one?"

I looked up to see Francesca extending a brown and white ball of fur in my direction. Scooping up the puppy, I held it in front of my face. After a thorough and slightly exaggerated once-over, I placed it in my lap.

"That is an excellent puppy," I declared. Despite it looking exactly identical to the last eight puppies she'd shoved my way. I was now covered in puppies and I couldn't tell one apart from any of the others.

"Yes, well, they are all excellent puppies," she replied with a fair amount of exasperation. "And Emery says they are all called Daisy. How shall I ever decide?"

I laughed at the seriousness of her tone. "In truth, I do not understand why they are all called Daisy, but I find it easier if we do not question Emery."

Francesca and I were visiting the stables of Laurel Park. Upon seeing the child's excitement over a new litter of puppies, Patty had said that she could pick one to have for her very own. Truthfully, Patty still worried over Francesca, and feared had been too many harmful secrets already in Francesca's short life. I refused to let the marquess and his choices negatively impact our lives ever again. My mother loved Franny as a grandmother should. We didn't wish for scandal to follow, nor make Franny question her place in our lives. We loved her, and that was enough.

"Look at my puppy, Patty!" Francesca's sweet voice rang out in excitement.

The adults all crowded around the child and dog as I approached.

"That looks like a lovely choice, Franny darling." Patty gave the child a gentle squeeze.

I slipped in behind Patty with a light touch on the small of her back. I could feel the warmth from her skin, and I ached to lean forward and place my lips on her neck, just beyond the collar of her day dress where a few blond tendrils had escaped.

"Well, hello there," she greeted as the others continued their inspection of the new puppy.

"Well, hello back, Duchess." I grinned.

"We thought you'd been attacked by puppies. You were gone for so long."

I laughed. "It was a very difficult decision. Franny wanted to assure the right one that they'd be going to a lovely family."

Patty's eyes softened at my words.

Our attention was drawn away when Silas asked suddenly, "Franny, what will you call your new puppy?"

The girl's dark brows lowered in confusion. "What do you mean? The dogs are all called Daisy. I shall have a little Daisy as well."

Nearly everyone groaned as Emery crowed her delight. "That is correct, dear Franny. You stick with your auntie Emery and I'll never steer you wrong."

"Please, no," Augustus murmured. "Do not encourage her."

Silas wore a sneaky smile that made me question the innocence of his original question. Especially when Emery met his eye and gave him a nudge with her elbow.

"Franny, you can name the puppy Daisy if you wish. You can name her whatever makes you happy." I gave the girl a smile that she returned.

"I would scold you for spoiling her." Patty's quiet words were whispered in my ear. "But I am no better, so I shall remain silent on the matter."

My laugh was interrupted as Francesca announced simply, "I think we should decide—the three of us—since she'll be coming to live with us. The puppy will be all of ours, not just mine. Right, Patty?"

The others quieted and turned soft looks our direction before Patty cleared her throat. "You're right. We'll decide together."

Francesca looked from me to Patty happily before nuzzling the sleepy animal and finding a seat on the plush blanket next to Genevieve.

"Right," sniffed Emery, attempting to master her emotions. "Shall we have some luncheon? I'll go and see if Mama and Father and Lady Salisbury would like to join us."

Augie smiled knowingly before strolling after his wife.

I settled on the blanket next to Patty, giving in to the urge and kissing her shoulder. "Are you all right?"

"Yes, of course," she answered quickly. I waited. "Just nervous about returning to London."

I nodded. "It will be fine. Franny likes living in town."

"I know," Patty admitted, eyes moving around those gathered. Her gaze snagged momentarily on Silas and Genevieve, both of whom were making Francesca double over with laughter. "How would you feel about acquiring a home here in Hampshire?" She looked back to me, and I was surprised to find uncertainty there. "I love visiting Laurel Park. I just thought it might be nice if we had our own space nearby. Perhaps we could visit the country more often if we had a home here as well. And I thought your mother might enjoy spending part of her time in the country if life in London grows difficult for her."

"I think that sounds like an excellent plan," I said sincerely.

"Really?"

"Yes." I laughed. "Why are you surprised?"

Patty scanned the gathering once more. "I don't know. They are *my* ridiculous family. I didn't want you to feel overwhelmed by all the Bartholomews."

Smiling, I pressed another kiss to her shoulder. "I rather think they are my ridiculous family as well."

"They are, aren't they?" Patty agreed, wistfulness in her tone. "But you wouldn't object to spending more time here? Truly?"

"Patty," I said, garnering her attention and making sure to meet her stare. "I am happy. In our life. In our marriage. And in our family. With you is where I want to be."

With a decisive nod, Patty replied, "All right."

"Besides, I am quite beloved by everyone here."

Patty snorted a laugh at that.

It was true. I got along famously with nearly anyone.

"I suppose that is accurate. You are friendly and affable to a fault. Has there ever been anyone who didn't immediately fall victim to your charms?"

"Just one," I admitted, raising a single brow in challenge.

"Oh!" Patty exclaimed as if abruptly recalling that she was, in fact, the lone holdout. Her sudden laughter had nearly everyone turning.

And I found I could hardly look away.

∼

Later that afternoon, I walked through the main stable of Kensworth Hall, the Duke of Kendrick's Hampshire estate and the neighboring home to Laurel Park. The day had been warm, and the earthy smells of the stable were both foreign and welcoming to a city dweller such as myself.

Emery and Augie were taking Francesca out on horseback. The girl was a lover of all animals and had particularly enjoyed learning to ride during our time in the country this summer.

Emery was an accomplished rider and made for an excellent teacher for Franny. She was also rather wild and spirited, so I felt grateful that Augustus would be joining them. I knew Patty appreciated that her sister and the duke had taken so well to Francesca. Emery loved referring to herself as "auntie" and it made Patty smile every time, without fail.

Patty and I had just met the duke and duchess in their stable, and after trying on several riding hats, we finally found the right size for Franny. I was in the tack room at the end of the main aisle putting away the unused items as the trio said their goodbyes to Patty in the yard.

After opening and closing several cabinets, I finally located the correct area for the supplies in the corner of the large space. I admired the various saddles and implements the grooms used for tending the horses here at Kensworth Hall. Perhaps I should speak to Augie about the stock they kept and where he acquired his thoroughbreds as well. It seemed like a fruitful investment opportunity. There was hardly an English gentleman without a stable full of horses.

Before I could ponder my future endeavors too thoroughly, Patty burst into the tack room. Positioned as I was in the corner behind the open door, she likely hadn't noticed me. Her back was to me as she braced her hands on the central worktable. I could see the elegant line of her back rising and falling with her deep, ragged breaths. Her attention was focused on the table as her shoulders slumped forward.

Her position was so similar to the first night we met that I spoke before I could question her reasons for escaping to this room. "You're not going to call me an arsehole, are you?"

Patty whirled at the sound of my voice, and when she spied me in the corner, I could see the emotion welling on her beautiful face.

"Patty," I breathed, moving toward her without thought.

"I'm all right," she assured me as I reached her, sliding an arm around her waist and cupping her cheek. "You just startled me."

"I'm sorry," I said, brushing away a tear that had escaped.

She huffed a laugh and shook her head. "I'm being silly. And luckily this time you are in no danger of being cursed for catching me during a weak moment."

"What happened?"

Her pale blue eyes were luminous when she spoke. "Franny called me Mum." My brows rose in surprise. "She was on her horse and just looked back at me and said, 'Goodbye, Mum. I'll be back soon.' She said it so simply and easily, and then she was gone."

Patty's voice cracked on the last word as she smiled, her countenance lightening until she fairly glowed.

I pulled her in close and wrapped my arms around her, so joyful in this moment. "That's wonderful, Patty. You are kind and thoughtful and loving. And so loyal and fierce. You would do anything for Franny. All of those things make you an amazing mother. She knows that."

I knew how Patty worried over the girl. We talked nearly every night before we slept about how we thought Francesca was adjusting or about some happy instance with the child that made us smile. But Patty also shared her concerns about the kind of life we were giving Francesca and her fears as a result. To have little Franny call her *Mum* today out of the clear blue sky, well, that was just excellent news.

"I'm so happy," Patty whispered into my ear, the confession rushed and barely audible, as if she feared the words might be snatched away by the wind, and her happiness along with it.

I smiled softly against her hair. "I am too."

"I didn't think it would ever be like this, Miles," she admitted, still holding tight to my embrace. "I thought I'd be angry and lonely forever. And then you..." She paused.

I could hear the emotion in her voice and feel her hitching breaths as her chest pressed tightly to my own. "And then I tricked you into a dance," I finished for her. "Two of them. And the rest is history. Well, actually, our very happy present. To be followed by an even happier future."

I felt her grip loosen as Patty pulled back slightly. Her gorgeous face came into focus as she stood before me. "I love you." She breathed the words, inscribing them onto my lips. Her kiss was slow and sweet as her hand came to my waist and pushed beneath the fabric of my coat.

I smiled against her mouth before murmuring my reply. "And I love you."

Patty backed away with a mischievous grin. She walked around to the door of the tack room and pushed it closed. With a definitive snick, she engaged the lock and turned to lean against the door, challenge in every line of her features.

"What's this, Duchess?" I asked, feigning confusion as I strolled toward her.

"We have some time before they return. I just thought…" Her voice trailed off as I leaned in, running my nose along the slender column of her throat.

I braced both hands on either side of her and pushed back to meet her gaze. "And you just thought you'd have your wicked way with me?"

Patty was fighting a smile. "That…" She leaned forward and pressed a kiss to my mouth before retreating. "Is exactly…" Another kiss. "What I thought."

She moved into the space I was keeping between us and pushed her chest into mine. Her soft, delicate curves had me already half hard in my trousers. When Patty reached down to cup my length, I fought a groan at her touch. She continued her ministrations, squeezing and rubbing me through my clothes as I removed my coat and tossed it on the table behind me.

I dove forward, capturing her mouth. Pulling insistently, I sucked on her bottom lip while I finally put my hands on her. Reaching around, I palmed her ass as I kissed her deeply. Patty matched my fervor, her tongue tangling with mine.

Everything about our movements felt urgent and necessary. We weren't simply fighting against time and privacy here in the stables. We were hungry and desperate for one another.

I'd always wanted Patty. Longed for her love and affection. And now that I had it, I would never let her go.

In a swift motion, I lowered my hands and grasped her thighs, lifting and turning to place her on the worktable. Without breaking our kiss, I pushed her skirts high around her waist. Patty's legs fell open wide as I found the slit in her drawers and pushed forward to find her warm, wet center. She moaned and dropped her head back as I massaged small circles near the juncture of her thighs, gathering her moisture and concentrating my efforts.

With her lips no longer in reach, I lowered my head and placed hot, wet kisses along her throat and chest as her breathing became choppy and uneven. With gentle strokes, I pushed in with two fingers while my thumb massaged her apex, focusing my attention on her sensitive center while my fingers thrust lazily in and out.

Patty surged forward and wrapped her arms around my shoulders. Resting her forehead against mine, she chanted, "Don't stop. God, don't stop."

Lost to the urgency in her voice, I kept my pace but increased the pressure to where all her pleasure seemed to concentrate. Patty moved against my hand and the feel of her walls tightening had my cock straining against my trousers. She gasped suddenly as her crisis struck, squeezing my fingers as she rode out her pleasure. I claimed her lips and swallowed down her moan, unwilling to share the sounds of her desire beyond these walls.

Before her breathing slowed, Patty reached down and unbuttoned the placket of my trousers. With a few firm strokes of her hand, I felt embarrassingly close to completion. However, my wife scooted forward, reaching the edge of the table before I pulled my fingers from her body and replaced them with my cock.

Patty wrapped her legs tightly around my waist as I braced my hands on the table and began to thrust. I pressed forward only to pull all the way back, loving the drag of my erection inside her tight channel. Patty's quiet moan drew my attention to her mouth. I kissed her then as I sped up my movements, feeling my body tightening with desire.

Forcing my mouth away, I said, "Touch yourself. Take what you need. I want to feel you come around me."

Patty eyed me before she leaned back slightly, using one hand to clutch the front edge of the table, while her other found the place where we were joined.

My thrusts became wilder as I watched her fingers, slippery and circling. When I saw her eyes close tightly and felt the pulse of her womanhood, I let myself go, movements jerky and unpracticed as I chased her release with my own.

As we clung to each other, breaths falling hot and uneven, I pressed a soft kiss to Patty's temple before whispering once more, "I love you, Duchess."

I watched the smile bloom across her delicate features as I disentangled myself and helped her down from the table. There were times I thought Patty was still surprised by what we had. That those simple words could catch her off guard and bring an unexpected smile to her face.

I couldn't really fathom how much my life had changed since my return to London. When I'd set foot on English soil, I'd merely been trying to exist. But now I felt like a man who could deserve someone like Patty. A person who had matured but still made mistakes. A man who was lucky enough to have been given a second chance and a brand-new start.

Once our clothes were back in order, and I picked a rebellious bit of straw from Patty's hair, I held out my arm. "Shall we go wait for our girl?"

"Not yet," she said, ignoring my arm and cupping my cheeks. After pressing a kiss both soft and adoring to my lips, she lingered, looking between my eyes before agreeing, "Now we're ready."

And I found that I was.

With her love and affection to carry me through, I was ready for whatever the day might bring.

Epilogue

PATTY

More than several years later

"Remind me why I am hosting a garden party again?"

"Because," Emery replied succinctly, "you are a duchess and can do whatever you wish." A pause. "And because no one else will let us attend events with our rambunctious children."

Truthfully, today's gathering was quite informal. Nearly all those attending were Bartholomews or had once been Bartholomews. And several close friends such as Mary and Daly would be joining us as well.

And surprising me with the request, Miles had invited the new owner of Brightleaf Farms, the horse breeder he'd invested in ages ago. He'd said the young man had recently taken over for his ailing uncle, and was brand new to London on business for the farm. Miles wanted to extend his welcome as he'd always been fond of the original owner and felt he owed the nephew his friendship by extension. I hadn't argued. If he wished to frighten the poor man with a Bartholomew gathering, he was welcome to it.

"Ah, yes. That's what it was," I agreed as Emery and Augie's eldest let out a bloodcurdling scream from somewhere beyond the hedgerows.

I bit my lip to hide my amusement.

My sister winced as the scream finally cut off. "I'm being punished for being so wild and willful in my youth."

I raised my brows but said nothing. Emery scowled and opened her mouth with a no-doubt pithy retort. But before she could, her husband came down the path hand in hand with their daughter Reeve, now four years of age, and little Beckett who had just turned two.

My sister's sigh was full of love and wonder. "Sometimes my heart simply cannot take it."

I knew the feeling.

Instinctively my eyes sought Miles. He was talking to someone near the gazebo. And never far from his side, there was our sweet Franny. She'd turned twelve recently and was very interested in both horses and fashion in equal measure, making both Emery and my mother exceedingly proud. Reaching down, Francesca absently dropped a treat that looked suspiciously like a bit of orange cake for Daisy, her faithful dog.

I shook my head but a smile tugged the corner of my lips. Our little family. Yes, sometimes my heart simply could not take it.

"I'm going to help Augie with our little beasts. Will you be all right?" Emery's voice brought my attention back to her as she straightened and pushed a loose pin into her coiffure.

"Of course," I said, glancing back to Miles. "I'll just join my husband. I should go and welcome the man with him. I believe that's the owner from the farm that he invited…" My voice trailed off as the stranger turned. I reached over and clasped Emery's wrist.

I could feel her shocked stare on my face, but I could not look away. *Oh, God. It couldn't be.*

With my eyes fixed on the man with my husband, I asked tightly, "Emery, where is Genevieve?"

"What is it?" I could see Emery's head twisting at the edge of my vision. "Gen is there, with Silas. Near the fountain."

"Go and get her. Make her help you with the children inside. Just keep her away until I can fix this."

"Patty, what is going on?" my sister whispered frantically. "Who do you— Oh no."

And now she'd seen him too. Taller than he'd ever been, with dark auburn hair reflecting the early autumn light. Julian Moore stood opposite my husband in a well-made suit and looked around the gardens with an expression I'd never seen on the boy's face.

"Go, Emery."

"Going!"

Emery took off toward the fountain, scooping up Beckett and grabbing Augie's hand on her way. I started toward the gazebo, keeping a cautious eye on Genevieve as I did so. She was still distracted by Silas. Thank God for my brother's endless attention-seeking.

This could not be happening. My poor sister.

It had been seven years since Julian had been sent away by his mother. I would never forget finding Genevieve that night at Laurel Park, crying on the floor of my old room, mourning the loss of her friend. I didn't know that she'd ever really recovered. The child I remembered, so bright-eyed and full of wonder, had hardened a bit after Julian's departure. She had clung to her writing, as I'd advised, and was wildly successful now as a result. But I also knew she'd never really given up on Jules. She'd written to him for years and never received a response. I thought something about his rejection had changed my sweet sister.

And now he was here, seven years later, quite unexpectedly.

With a final glance toward the fountain, I saw Emery and her party join Gen and Silas. I sighed in relief just as I approached the gazebo.

Francesca spied me first, eyes alight. "Papa, look!"

Miles turned a devastating smile my way, but must have read something in my expression because his brows lowered in concern. I feared my panic over Julian and Genevieve had alerted my husband to some crisis. I didn't want him to worry, however. So I pasted a bright smile on my face and came to stand next to him and Francesca. I reached out and gave her shoulder a gentle squeeze as Daisy pressed eager paws to my dark skirts.

"Patty, I want to introduce you to the new owner of Brightleaf Farms," Miles said smoothly. "This is Mr. Moore. He's enjoying his first visit to London to meet with buyers and investors. Mr. Moore, this is my wife, Patricia, the Duchess of Cawthorn."

With an expression that felt equal parts nostalgic for the young boy I'd once been so fond of and terribly fierce due to the pain he'd caused my sister, I met Mr. Moore's gaze quite coolly. It seemed the ferocious sister had won out.

"Hello, Julian. What an unexpected surprise."

∽

Genevieve and Julian's story, *Third Degree Yearn*, is coming June 27, 2023! Pre-order Today!

About the Author

Laney Hatcher is a firm believer that there is a spreadsheet for every occasion and pie is always the answer. She is an author of stories that have a past, in a language of love that's universal. Often too practical for her own good, Laney enjoys her life in the southern United States with her husband, children, and incredibly entitled cat.

Find Laney Hatcher online:
Facebook: https://bit.ly/3s6KnuY
Newsletter: https://bit.ly/3sUGwAk
Amazon: https://amzn.to/3IaOwU7
Instagram: https://bit.ly/3s4IRcS
Website: https://laneyhatcher.com/
Goodreads: https://bit.ly/3BD0Gme
TikTok: https://www.tiktok.com/@laneyhatcherauthor

Also by Laney Hatcher

Bartholomew Series

First to Fall: A Friends to Lovers Historical Romance

Second Chance Dance: An Enemies to Lovers Historical Romance

Third Degree Yearn: A Second Chance Historical Romance

Smartypants Romance

London Ladies Embroidery Series

Neanderthal Seeks Duchess: A Smartypants Romance Out of this World Title

Well Acquainted: A Smartypants Romance Out of this World Title

Printed in Great Britain
by Amazon